Her heart thudded in her chest as she waited for something to happen.

The first gunshot caused her to jump. As the shots intensified, she heard shouting. She recognized Ryan's rich, deep voice ordering someone to lay down a weapon.

Kitty moved toward the broken window and peered out. The bullet that flew past her head came so close that it created a breeze and she screamed, dropping to the floor again. The bullets wouldn't stop coming.

She stood and ran into the hallway, intending to gain a better vantage point upstairs, but pain sliced into her leg like a bee sting, and she fell to the floor. The gunshots gradually ceased.

"Kitty," Ryan yelled into the house. "Where are you?"

"I'm here."

He appeared at her side.

"My leg," she said. "Something hit my leg."

He inspected her right thigh, where blood was trickling. "A bullet grazed you," he said. "It's not serious."

"When will it be over?" she cried.

"Soon. We'll get through this, Kitty," he said soothingly. "I promise."

As much as she wanted to believe his promises, she wasn't sure she could.

Only time would tell.

Elisabeth Rees was raised in the Welsh town of Hay-on-Wye, where her father was the parish vicar. She attended Cardiff University and gained a degree in politics. After meeting her husband, they moved to the wild rolling hills of Carmarthenshire, and Elisabeth took up writing. She is now a full-time wife, mother and author. Find out more about Elisabeth at elisabethrees.com.

INNOCENT
TARGET

ELISABETH REES

HARLEQUIN® LOVE INSPIRED® SUSPENSE

Recycling programs for this product may not exist in your area.

LOVE INSPIRED BOOKS

ISBN-13: 978-1-335-67885-0

Innocent Target

www.Harlequin.com

Printed in U.S.A.

And the light shineth in darkness;
and the darkness comprehended it not.
–John 1:5

For Shana and Jack Asaro and baby Natalie,
with a wish that many blessings are bestowed upon
their newly grown family.

ONE

The air inside the house was heavy and moist, the result of an unseasonably warm day in an Oklahoma winter that was likely to result in a thunderstorm. In the living room of her home, Kitty Linklater wiped her brow with a cool cloth, holding it to her temple and sighing. She'd worked up a sweat after sitting at her computer for almost five hours, writing her latest article for the county newspaper, the *Comanche Times*. She read the headline aloud: "'Bethesda Man Challenges His Murder Conviction.'" Hovering her finger over the send button, she hesitated, knowing that the article was controversial, likely to enrage the townsfolk and increase her unpopularity.

But Kitty was no stranger to controversy or unpopularity. For twelve months, she had been investigating the murder of a local teenage girl, found at the side of the road two years previously, her body callously burned to destroy evidence. The small town of Bethesda had reeled from the brutality of it and the residents breathed a collective sigh of relief when a man was arrested, tried and convicted of the crime. Kitty was the only person to feel devastated, because that convicted man was her beloved father, Harry, and she was now utilizing her skills as a freelance investigative journalist to try to prove his innocence. She had initially placed her faith in the justice system, hoping that the truth would win the day, but after the verdict was announced, she knew she had to begin her own investigation.

Her cell phone rang in her pocket, shrill and sharp, causing her black cat, Shadow, to jump from her lap. He ran from the room indignantly, swishing his tail.

She pulled the cell from her jeans. "Hello."

"Hey, Kitty." The voice belonged to Sarah Willis, editor of the *Comanche Times*. "You're late on your deadline."

Kitty was given a weekly slot in the paper, trusted by Sarah to fill it with a mix of investigative coverings and opinion pieces on the most interesting and significant stories in the county.

"It's done," she said. "I'm about to send it to you now."

"What is it? Please tell me you've moved on from the Bethesda murder."

"I wrote another piece about my father being

wrongfully accused." She ignored the groan on the other end of the line. "It's an important story. I have to cover it."

"No, you don't, Kitty," Sarah said strongly. "This is the third time you've subbed a piece about your father. It's not right. You can't continue to use the paper to push your own agenda."

"I know it looks bad, but this could be a huge story. I uncovered some new evidence that supports my dad's claim of innocence."

"You did?"

"I managed to track down a guy who was in the Starlight Bar on the night of the murder. You remember that's where my father spent the entire evening when the girl was murdered?"

"And he spent the entire evening there because he's an alcoholic, right?"

"That's not relevant," she retorted. She was sick of people judging her father because of his addiction. "The guy from the bar says he definitely saw my dad there and he's willing to go on record as a witness."

"Is this guy also an alcoholic?"

Kitty recalled the man's ruddy complexion, his shaking hands and his rotting teeth. "Probably, but that doesn't make him a liar."

"No, but it makes him an unreliable witness. There were four men besides your dad in the

Starlight Bar on that night and none of them could validate his alibi in court, right?"

Kitty had been over this a million times before: aside from her father, there had been three drinkers in the bar, plus the owner and bartender, Harvey Flynn. Of the three drinkers, one had died of liver disease, one—the man she'd found—was an out-of-towner the police couldn't find, and the third had no memory of the evening due to excess alcohol consumption. Only Harvey Flynn was ruled to be a credible, available witness and he claimed not to have seen Kitty's father all evening.

"I know what you're going to say, Sarah," Kitty said. "A jury convicted my father on the evidence, but this new witness just might be enough to throw the conviction into doubt."

"Listen to me." Sarah's voice was sympathetic, but Kitty knew her boss was exasperated. "After your last piece about your father went out, I received a ton of complaints from people in Bethesda. They don't want you reminding them of what happened to that poor girl. This is the last time I'll allow you to submit an article about the murder."

Kitty pinched the bridge of her nose. Since her father's incarceration, she'd been spending a huge amount of time investigating the gruesome crime, neglecting her paid journalistic work. The *Comanche Times* was one of very few steady sources of income and she couldn't afford to lose it. Until recently she'd housed a tenant in the self-contained apartment attached to the house, but he'd moved out two weeks ago, and money was tight.

"Okay, I understand," she said finally.

"Great. Give me your latest piece and I'll get it in tomorrow's edition."

Kitty clicked off the phone, walked to the open window and gazed at the beautiful Chinese pistache tree in the yard. Her father had planted the tree ten years ago as a memorial to Kitty's mother, after cancer had stolen her from them. Her death had been the catalyst for Harry's drinking, the coping mechanism he had so recklessly chosen in his grief.

A floorboard creaked above and Kitty called out to her little black cat. He would no doubt be hungry, having waited patiently for his dinner while his mistress furiously tapped on a keyboard.

"Shadow," she called. "I have some nice fish for you."

She went into the kitchen, retrieving a plastic tub of cod fillets from the fridge and turning on the radio for company. She was beginning to feel terribly lonely in her lakeside house, set in beautiful woodland but secluded and isolated.

There was another floorboard creak overhead. "Come on, Shadow. Where are you?"

A meow sounded at her feet and her cat wound himself through her legs. She froze for a second, a lump building in her throat. If Shadow was here, then who or what was upstairs?

She swallowed hard, telling herself not to panic. She put down the tub of fish and walked into the hallway, peering up the staircase.

"Hello?" she said tentatively. "Is somebody here?"

As a precaution, she took her cell from her pocket and punched in 9-1-1. She didn't intend to actually place the call, but it didn't hurt to be ready, just in case.

Ascending the stairs, Kitty kept her ears attuned to any sounds. A sudden noise made her jump. Flattening her back against the wall in the upstairs hallway, she placed a hand over her heart to try and steady it, telling herself that there must be a rational explanation for the sound, like an object falling to the floor.

"There's no one here, there's no one here," she chanted, as if repeating these words would calm her nerves.

She then thought of the small figurine that she kept on her dresser by the window in her bedroom, a gift from her parents for her eighth birthday. Maybe the new drapes had gotten caught in the wind and knocked it onto the rug.

Pushing open her bedroom door, she went into the neat and orderly room. There on the floor was her little figurine, lying on its side beneath the open window, exactly as she had suspected. She stooped to retrieve it just as the door slammed shut behind her with an almighty bang. She sprang up and swiveled around. There was a man standing just a few feet away, a ski mask covering his face, a long-bladed knife in his hand. She screamed, but he remained as still as a statue, his chest rising and falling with heavy breathing.

"Wh-what do you want?" she managed to stutter.

His chilling reply let her know that this wasn't a burglar.

"I want to kill you."

She replied with the only thing that came to her terrified mind. "Why?"

"Because you wouldn't leave well enough alone," he said, advancing toward her.

She began to back away. "What do you mean?"

"You should've accepted that your father killed Molly."

"But I know he didn't."

"You know too much," the man said. "And that's why you must die."

He lunged with his knife. She had no time to think. There was a gun in her dresser, but she had no opportunity to retrieve it. She grabbed the nearest thing to hand, a vase of flowers, and hurled it at the man's head. The heavy glass bounced off his shoulder and he yelled a curse word, dropping his knife. Kitty tried to snatch the handle but he was too quick for her. Within seconds, the weapon was back in his grasp and she was again at his mercy.

Then she remembered the cell in her hand and hit the call button with her thumb, backing away to the open window. Not daring to bring the cell to her ear, she heard the emergency operator's faint voice, asking which service was required.

"Police," she yelled. "62 Lakeside Drive, Bethesda. There's an intruder."

Her rear end was now against the windowsill. There was nowhere to go except through the opening. She turned and leaped from the room, out into the clear air, landing in a jumble of limbs and leaves of the old oak tree. She tumbled down, hitting branches as she went, which knocked the breath from her lungs. Her cell flew from her hand and she came to rest on the grass with a thump. She was sore and scratched, but not seriously injured.

She looked up and saw the man leaning through the window, watching her haul herself to her knees. For a brief moment he appeared to be considering descending the same way as she had, but then changed his mind and disappeared from view. That meant he intended to reach her via the stairs, which would take only a matter of seconds. She picked herself up and ran toward the main road, not daring to look back or imagine what would happen if she failed to outrun this wild attacker.

"Help!" she screamed into the empty woods. "Please somebody help me."

Chief Deputy Ryan Lawrence surveyed the quiet street outside the station. When he'd taken the job as the chief deputy at the Bethesda station one week ago, nobody had warned him it would be so quiet. His hometown of Lawton, with its almost one hundred thousand residents, was huge in comparison to this little town of barely three thousand. He'd agreed to transfer to the small satellite office in order to take a promotion that would put him in line for the sheriff's election in a few months' time. He just hoped that landing his dream job as county sheriff was worth the endless monotony of this sleepy town.

The radio clipped to his belt crackled to life: "We've got a report from Kitty Linklater of an intruder at 62 Lakeside Drive. Immediate assistance required."

He grabbed the radio and spoke into it as he retrieved the truck keys from the hook. "I'm on it."

Ryan raced along the road that led to the Linklater home—the former residence of the murderer Harry Linklater. It was the place where Harry's daughter had dreamed up ridiculous notions of proving her father's innocence and freeing him from prison. Ryan had hoped he'd be able to steer clear of this misguided woman, but she apparently needed his help, so his personal feelings would have to be put to one side.

He knew that Kitty was deeply unpopular in these parts, reviled for her unwavering support of her father and regarded as sullying the memory of the murdered girl through her newspaper articles questioning the jury's verdict. Molly Thomas had been a gifted musician and a straight A student, a girl whose only mistake had been to accept a lift from Harry Linklater when hitchhiking to a party. Molly's last known words were a text to a friend: Catching a ride with Mr. Linklater, see you in ten minutes. But she never made it to the party and was found dead a few hours later. Molly's untimely death had shattered the whole county, and now perhaps someone wanted vengeance.

He turned onto the lane that led to the lake, instantly seeing a woman who he assumed was Kitty sprinting in his direction, covered in leaves and twigs, blood trickling down her face. And behind her was a man dressed in jeans and a hoodie, a ski mask covering his face. Ryan slammed on his brakes to avoid hitting Kitty, jumped from the truck and raised his gun at the suspect.

"Stop right there," he commanded, pointing his weapon. "You're under arrest."

Kitty stood in the lane, her eyes wide with fear, her hands trembling at her sides. The masked man stopped dead, looking between Ryan and the lake, as if assessing his escape routes. Then he turned and ran toward the water, a blade glinting in his hand.

Ryan gave immediate chase.

He was gaining ground on the suspect, but not enough to buy him the time he needed. When the man reached the jetty, he jumped into a small wooden boat and used the blade in his hand to quickly cut the mooring rope. He then activated the motor and pushed it to maximum throttle, sending a wash of water cascading onto the pebbles along the shoreline. Ryan came to a halt and could do nothing but watch as the intruder made his escape over the glittering lake.

Ryan holstered his weapon and walked back

to Kitty, finding her sitting in the passenger seat of his truck, staring straight ahead, shock written across her face. He slid into the driver's seat.

"I'm Chief Deputy Ryan Lawrence from the sheriff's office in Bethesda," he said. "Are you Kitty Linklater?"

She nodded.

"I'm sorry to say that your intruder escaped across the lake," he continued. "Can you tell me exactly what happened here?"

Her voice shook with emotion. "Somebody is trying to kill me."

"Did he hurt you? Do you need medical attention?"

"I'm not hurt," Kitty replied. "At least not physically, anyway."

He studied her face. Her eyes were the darkest brown, a perfect match for her hair, and set in an exotic and striking face. It was a cliché, but she had movie-star looks, reminding him of a young Sophia Loren. Yet her clothes were anything but glamorous. She wore threadbare old jeans and an oversize shirt, both of which appeared to be torn from a scuffle or a fall.

"Why do think that this man is trying to kill you?" he asked, flipping open his notepad. "Try to stay calm and tell me all the relevant details."

"I've been investigating the murder of Molly Thomas in an effort to prove that my father couldn't possibly have done it," she said. "And now that I'm getting closer to the truth, the real killer wants me dead."

He nodded silently, pushing down a sudden rush of anger. Murderers like Harry Linklater always denied their crimes. Ryan had seen it all before. The monster who'd killed his sister, Gina, when she was only nine years of age had protested his innocence for almost twenty years. Despite overwhelming forensic evidence against him, Cody Jones had repeatedly tried to appeal his conviction, with no success. It was only twelve months ago that Jones had finally admitted his guilt in the hope of securing a successful parole hearing. Men like this were liars, manipulators and tricksters. And Harry Linklater was no different.

Ryan's distaste must have shown on his face, giving his feelings away.

"You don't believe me, do you?" she said, a note of resignation in her voice. "You think my father's guilty, just like the rest of this town does."

Ryan recalled being drafted from Lawton two years earlier to assist with the forensic sweep of the area where Molly had been found dead. He had arrived before the body was moved and it was a sight that would haunt him forever. Harry had attempted to burn Molly's remains to destroy the evidence, but it wasn't quite enough to cover his tracks.

"It doesn't much matter what I think," he replied, reaching for a first aid box in the glove compartment. "Because a jury found your father guilty and he's now serving his time. I'm not interested in protecting your father, Miss. Linklater. I'm interested in protecting *you*. So let's stick to the facts of the matter, okay?"

He took a wad of tissue from the first aid box and held it to her forehead, where a small cut was bleeding.

"The fact of the matter is that this man wants me dead," she said, taking the tissue from his hand and applying her own pressure instead. "Because he wants to hide the truth about Molly's death. It's proof that my dad is innocent."

Ryan didn't buy this one bit. Proof involved actual evidence—evidence like traces of Molly's blood on the seats of Harry's car and his total lack of verifiable alibi. Harry was guilty. Everyone but Kitty knew it.

She stared him down. "I don't expect you to believe me, but I know I'm onto something, and when I finally prove that my father was wrongfully imprisoned, I'll happily accept an apology from you, Chief Deputy Lawrence."

With the blood drying on her face and her eyes blazing, she had the appearance of a soldier straight from the battlefield. And he was quietly impressed by her resolve. But he had no desire to indulge her fantasies of her father's victimhood. There was only one victim in this scenario and she was buried in Bethesda town cemetery.

"I can promise you that I'll thoroughly investigate this attack and do all I can to bring the perpetrator to justice," he said, starting up the truck. "So why don't we drive on down to your house, where I can take a full statement from you. Are you okay with that?"

"Yes, sir."

"Please call me Ryan. May I call you Kitty?"

She shrugged, which he took to be an affirmative answer. Dark clouds had been gathering in the sky for hours and he heard the first distant rumble of thunder. There seemed to be electricity in the air, sparking an atmosphere inside the truck, building to an inevitable storm.

Kitty sat in the kitchen, checking her statement, while the new deputy thoroughly scanned the house and yard for any clues regarding the intruder's identity. He walked into the kitchen with a solemn expression. The peals of thunder had intensified and a quick, sharp flash occasionally lit up the room.

"Well, at least this storm should clear the air,"

he said, sitting down at the table. "Are you happy with the statement?"

She nodded while sliding it over to him.

"Do you live alone?" he asked.

"Yes."

"I noticed that you have a separate apartment here. I thought you might have a tenant, perhaps."

"I did," she said. "But he decided to leave after some of the townsfolk told him he shouldn't be associating with me." She picked at a worn spot on the table with her fingernail. "I'm a social outcast, you see. Frank Price at the hardware store even started a petition to have me banned from Main Street."

"While I don't approve of that kind of petition, the town has every right to object to your antics."

"My antics?" she questioned, folding her arms. "And just what is that supposed to mean?"

His green eyes rested on her face for a long time, impossible to read. His red hair and freckled skin gave him a boyish appearance, but those eyes were definitely grown-up and sensible.

"Nobody wants to believe there could be a murderer in their family," he said. "And I understand what you must be going through—"

She put up her hand to cut him off. "Hold on a minute. How could you possibly understand what I'm going through?"

"My sister was murdered by a stranger when she was only nine years old," he said, his eye contact unwavering. "Being that close to such a brutal crime is tough. It never leaves you."

She bowed her head, a sour taste spreading in her mouth.

"I'm sorry," she whispered. "I'm really sorry."

"The man who killed my sister is in prison serving a life sentence, so at least we got to see justice done."

Despite his efforts to sound fair and avoid condemning her, Kitty knew that, just like the rest of the townsfolk, he probably viewed her actions as pointless and misguided, the *antics* of a loyal daughter, brainwashed to trust her father wholeheartedly.

"It's good that you got to see justice done," she said, deciding to be bold. "But justice hasn't been served for Molly. Her killer is still out there."

She noticed the flare of his nostrils, the clench of his jaw, and she knew that she had correctly identified him as a disapprover. Ryan moistened his lips as a flash of lightning streaked across the sky behind him, followed by the low rumble a few seconds later.

He leaned over the table on his forearms, fingers intertwined. "Your continued investigation into a crime that's already been solved is rubbing people the wrong way. Someone might have gotten so riled up that he's looking to punish you for it."

She was incredulous. "Are you saying it's my fault someone tried to kill me?"

"Absolutely not. You have the right to ask questions and print newspaper articles and challenge the jury's decision to convict. You have the right to do all of those things without fear of repercussions, but I'm just asking you to consider whether it's in your interest to continue pushing your opinion on people." He pulled a small twig from her hair. "I really don't want to see you get seriously hurt."

She picked up her empty coffee mug and walked to the sink to rinse it out.

"I have to take that risk," she said, her back to him. "I don't expect you to understand and I don't even expect you to care, but I know that my father didn't kill Molly. He gave her a ride to a party at the Suttons' farm after she'd fallen at the side of the road and cut her knees. That was why her blood was in his car. He left her alive and well at the bottom of the lane that leads to the farmhouse."

She watched Ryan's reflection in the kitchen window, rubbing his neck and giving an almost imperceptible shake of his head.

"I guess it sounds crazy to you," she continued. "You see my dad as just another ex-con who'll say anything to pass the blame on to someone else. Plus, I'm guessing you know that he served time in prison for armed robbery when he was eighteen."

Ryan nodded.

"He changed his ways a long time ago. He's not a bad person."

"From what I understand, he tied up two people at a post office and threatened them with a shotgun before robbing the place. Is that correct?"

Kitty ran a hand through her hair, gathering the strands in her fist and gripping them tight in frustration. "That was thirty-five years ago. Don't you think people can change?"

Ryan scraped his chair on the linoleum as he stood. "Like I already said, I'm more concerned about you than your father. I don't like the thought of you being here all alone." He shifted on his feet, fingering the edges of his hat. "So I might have a potential solution."

She turned around and leaned against the sink. "You do?"

"I've been commuting eighty miles from Lawton and it's pretty tiring, so I'd rather live closer to the station. I've been looking for a room to rent."

She smiled wryly as she realized what he was getting at. "You want to rent the apartment?"

"It would mean I'm only ten minutes from work, and I can be here on hand in case your attacker comes back."

She said nothing for a while, listening to the clatter of raindrops on the deck outside. This man had admitted that he thought her father guilty. Could she stand to share living space with someone who so openly doubted her father's innocence? All she wanted was for one person to believe her, just one single individual to support her investigation. When Ryan had rushed to her aid, she had briefly hoped he might be that person, but now those hopes were dashed.

"You should know that I use this house to coordinate the campaign to free my father," she said. "So if you're likely to be offended by that, you should look for another place."

"I don't share your opinion," he said calmly. "But I'm not offended by it."

She wanted to shout and scream, to tell him that her opinion was correct. But doing so would be a pointless waste of energy.

"Some of the townsfolk might turn on you," she added. "Lodging here could seriously damage your reputation."

"My reputation can take the hit," he said.

"Please don't worry about me, Kitty. You're the main concern here."

She had to make a decision either way. She would feel safer with someone else here. And the electricity bill was overdue. "When would you like to move in?"

"Tomorrow afternoon?"

She swallowed her doubts and took the plunge. "Okay. I'll get the place ready for you."

"Thank you. I appreciate it."

Following him to the front door, she said, "The only thing missing from the apartment is a kitchen, so you'll have to share mine. Maybe we could decide on a roster so we won't get in each other's way."

"I won't get in your way. You won't even know I'm here."

Somehow, she doubted that very much.

"Lock all the windows and doors when I'm gone," he said. "And if the intruder returns, call me immediately." He handed her a card containing his contact details. "Even if it's the middle of the night."

She took the card, rubbing her finger over the embossed lettering of Chief Deputy Ryan Lawrence, and watched him sprint through the rain to his truck. The air temperature had plummeted with the storm and she shivered, feeling the sinister presence of her masked attacker all around her.

The intruder would return. Of that she was sure. The only question was when.

TWO

"You're doing what?" Deputy Shane Harmon slapped his thigh while doubling over with laughter. "You're renting an apartment at the Linklater house? You sure must be a glutton for punishment. Some people say that she's bad news."

Ryan bristled at the criticism of Kitty. She might be mistakenly loyal to her father, but she was a good and decent person underneath it all. After a lot of reflection, he'd concluded that her heart was in the right place. He only wished that her head would overrule her strong emotions.

"Come on now, Shane, she's not that bad," Ryan said. "She's had a rough couple of years, what with all the publicity about her father's crime, and now she's convinced that somebody is trying to kill her."

"Kill her?" Shane questioned with a dubious frown. "She's not exactly Bethesda's favorite person, but I don't think anybody would want her dead."

"Well, someone certainly tried to hurt her yesterday. I chased him to a boat on the lake, which I'd like you to try to trace."

"There are a lot of boats that use the lake, so it'll be tough to locate the owner," Shane said. "Does Kitty have any idea who it might be?"

"No, but she reckons the attack is linked to her investigation into the Molly Thomas murder."

Shane pinched his lips together in disgust. "The Molly Thomas murder is solved. Can't we just let that little girl rest in peace, so her family can try to move on?"

"You won't hear any argument from me on that," Ryan said, instantly conjuring up an image of his parents, and how hard the loss of Gina had been on them. If anyone had been around, constantly talking about the trial, trying to cast doubt on the conviction, it would have destroyed their tattered peace of mind. "But Kitty's got it in her head that the real killer is trying to stop her from getting to the truth."

"The only truth is that Kitty's made enemies around here, asking all her intrusive questions and publishing newspaper articles criticizing our police work. If somebody is targeting her, she's only got herself to blame. She needs to stop what she's doing or else she might come to real harm."

"That's not fair," Ryan stated. "She's not doing anything illegal and she has the right to live in peace, just like everyone else. We don't have to agree with her, but it's our sworn duty to protect her."

"Yes, sir." Shane appeared contrite. "I guess I went too far there. It's a touchy subject, but you're right that she shouldn't be afraid to speak her mind. But she's not the only outspoken one in this town. I just hope you know what you're doing by renting her apartment." He nodded to the street, where some residents were making their way to the station, faces fixed with angry expressions. "Because when these folk hear that you're rooming with Kitty, they won't be happy."

Before he could reply, the door opened and Frank Price walked in with his grandson, Buzz.

Frank was the owner of the hardware store and Buzz was just eighteen, recently graduated from high school and now working for his granddad. Close behind the two men were Carla Torlioni and her husband, Joe, from the café. And all were carrying copies of the *Comanche Times*.

Frank slapped the newspaper on the counter. "We need you to put a stop to Kitty Linklater."

Ryan read the headline at the top of the page the paper was opened to: "Bethesda Man Challenges His Murder Conviction." He scanned the story below, learning that Kitty had tracked down a man who could corroborate her father's alibi on the night in question. Apparently, Molly's time of death had been approximately 11:00 p.m., whereas a new witness placed Harry in the Starlight Bar from 8:00 p.m. until 2:00 a.m. From the looks of the man's photo, visible in the corner of the article, he was a heavy drinker and possibly a transient, not exactly a model witness.

"That poor Thomas family has been through quite enough," Carla said. "It's not right."

There were murmurs of agreement from all present in the station, even from Shane. Ryan could understand why. If somebody had been fighting to undermine the conviction of Cody Jones, he would've fought against it with the same level of resentment. What Kitty was doing was perhaps morally wrong.

But it wasn't illegal. And it was his job to uphold only the law.

"I'm afraid there's nothing that can be done about Kitty's investigation," Ryan said. "She's perfectly entitled to make these claims, whether we like it or not."

"So you're saying we just have to put up with it?" Carla said.

"Why don't you complain to the newspaper people?" he suggested. "They're the ones printing the articles."

"We've already done that," Frank said. "But we want someone with official authority to get involved. You're meant to keep order around here, so do something."

"And just what would you suggest I do?" Ryan asked, a little perplexed. "Arrest her? For what?"

"Can't you warn her to stop stirring up trouble?" Frank asked. "Why can't Kitty move away and leave us in peace? It'd be nice to see the entire Linklater family gone from these parts."

"This is Kitty's town, too, and I don't think she has any intention of going anywhere." Ryan wondered if he should let the townsfolk know of his new living arrangements, but decided that now was not a good time. "I hope nobody thinks they can force Kitty out of her family home. She was attacked by a masked man yesterday, and I'm very concerned for her safety. If anyone knows anything about this attack, I'd appreciate you sharing that information."

The station fell quiet.

Carla was the first to break the silence. She cleared her throat importantly and adjusted the collar on her starched white blouse.

"I'm sorry that Kitty's been attacked, I really am, but she's got to take some responsibility for her actions. Plenty of people don't take kindly to her meddling."

Joe was clearly more sympathetic than his

wife. "Come on, honey, we don't wish harm on her, do we?" He turned to Ryan as Carla gave her husband a stony glare. "Is Kitty okay?"

"She's fine," he replied. "But she's pretty shaken up. Whatever Kitty's father has done, she doesn't deserve to fear for her life, so if any of you hear about who might be responsible for the attack yesterday, I'd like you to come and talk with me in confidence. We can't allow residents to take the law into their own hands." He caught Buzz's eye. "Isn't that right, young man?"

"Yes, sir," Buzz said compliantly.

With a head of fair curls and baby blue eyes, Buzz possessed a face more suited to a boy band heartthrob than a hardware store clerk. But he was clearly cowed by his grandfather and his body language was uneasy.

"I hear that Sheriff Wilkins is retiring soon," Frank said to Ryan. "And I've been told that you're a hot contender for the job. But if you don't get Kitty under control then your chances of support from this town don't look good."

Ryan frowned, unhappy with Frank's choice of words. Kitty wasn't a wayward animal to be brought *under control*. She was a human being, acting irrationally because she loved her father.

"Let's go, Buzz," Frank said, leading his grandson to the door. "I'm sure our new chief deputy has got a lot of work to do."

The four residents filed from the station, leaving Ryan to contemplate just how he was going to broach this subject with Kitty. Shane was already one step ahead of him.

"I wouldn't want to be in your shoes, trying to persuade Kitty Linklater to drop her investigation," he said. "She won't take kindly to you telling her what to do."

"I don't intend to tell her what to do. I just need to remind her that she has a responsibility to be kind to the community. They're hurting."

"She's hurting, too, boss. And people in pain tend to lash out when cornered."

Ryan rubbed a hand down his face and sighed. That was exactly what he was worried about.

Kitty walked around her house, checking that each window was closed and locked. She fingered the Band-Aid covering the cut on her forehead, pressing down the sides, feeling a bruise settling there.

On top of her worries about her attacker, she was also anxious about Ryan moving in to the apartment. She kept telling herself that his presence would be reassuring, but a more powerful emotion niggled away: dread. For months she had been increasingly rejected by a small but vocal section of the community. Most of the town was holding its peace on the issue, but those few voices kept getting louder—and there was no one actively on her side, speaking up in her defense. As a result, she'd become ever more reclusive, avoiding town functions and special events. But now she would possibly be forced to confront the hostility that she expertly evaded in her daily life. Ryan was quite open about his belief in her father's guilt and the more she considered this fact, the more it bothered her. For a lawmaker, he was closed-minded and biased, not willing to even consider that the jury made the wrong call. Of course, she knew why. A man who'd lost his sister to a murderer at the tender age of nine would never trust the word of a convicted killer. She would simply have to live with his prejudiced mind and try not to let it bother her.

She entered the living room, jumping at a streak of black in her peripheral vision.

"Oh, Shadow," she said in playful rebuke, seeing him walking along the windowsill outside, crying to come in. "Why don't you use your flap like a normal cat? Okay," she said, opening the window. "Come on in and get dry."

He snaked through the window, walked onto the piano and shook himself over her, causing her to laugh and brush herself down. Then she reached for the handle of the window to close it up.

But someone was waiting for her.

A hand stretched up from below and firmly clasped her wrist, pulling her forward. She reacted instantly and instinctively, yanking her arm from side to side as if to shake off a spider. She looked for any indicators that would help her identify this man, but Kitty could see only a limb, an arm that belonged to a man hidden in the bush below.

Using her other hand, she pulled the window shut while simultaneously wrenching her arm inside. The frame caught the hairy limb of her attacker and he howled from below, losing his grip and pulling back, allowing her to fully shut the window. She secured the latch, turned the lock and ran from the room, snatching up her cell from the hallway table along the way.

She could hear the door being rattled as she fumbled in her pocket for Ryan's number.

"Ryan," she said breathlessly when he answered. "Somebody's here again. He's trying to get in."

"Stay calm and I'll be there soon."

A bullet came through the front door, slamming hard into the wall just yards away. She screamed.

"He's shooting!" she cried.

"I'm on my way right now," he promised. "Do you have a gun?"

She ran up the stairs. "Yes, it's in my bedroom."

Another bullet zinged through the air behind her, finding a vase on the table and shattering it into pieces.

Ryan clearly heard the commotion. "Get your gun, stay upstairs and barricade yourself in your room. Can you do that?"

"Yes."

"Don't be afraid to shoot, okay?"

"Okay."

"Hold tight."

She gasped, remembering that Shadow was still in the living room. Without hesitation, she ran back down the stairs, screaming as another bullet pinged through the door, just missing her shoulder.

"Shadow," she called. "Where are you?"

He immediately ran to the sound of her voice and she scooped him up into her arms. Then she turned and raced back to her room, as a pounding foot came down on the wooden door from outside, pummeling it.

Reaching her bedroom, she fled inside and slammed the door. After placing Shadow on the floor, Kitty used all her force to drag her dresser across the entrance, wondering if it would be enough. She figured the front door must have given way when she heard a loud bang resound through the house, and then footsteps run through the downstairs area.

"Please hurry, Ryan," she muttered, dragging her bed across the rug to give her barricade extra strength.

The footsteps stopped. Her noise had revealed her location. Now her attacker would surely be coming for her. She slid open the top drawer of her low dresser and pulled out her black handgun, checking the bullets in the chamber. The man was there, outside her room, rattling the handle, trying to force it open.

"I have a gun," she shouted as a warning. "And I'm not afraid to shoot."

Silence.

Was he still there? Her heart was in her mouth as the seconds ticked by.

Then he began to kick the door, sending her dresser skipping forward a little each time. She raised her gun, aimed it at the door, closed her eyes and squeezed the trigger. Her bullet went right through the door, leaving a perfectly circular hole.

The kicking ceased. Had she hit him? Was he injured or worse? She repositioned the dresser securely against the door and waited. Shadow seemed to understand the danger and had hidden himself away beneath the bed.

The sound of a siren wafted in the distance.

Kitty dropped to her knees with a groan of thanks. Immediately, she heard her attacker's footsteps pounding down the staircase, scurrying away. As the siren grew louder, she gained enough confidence to heave the bed, then the dresser away, from the door and squeeze through the gap. From the top of the stairs, she saw the front door off its hinges lying on the hallway floor, pounded into pieces.

As she stared at the open doorway, it filled with Ryan's figure, gun in hand, concern etched on his face.

"He's gone," she said.

"Are you okay?"

She nodded, biting the inside of her lip and blinking fast. She wasn't okay and it didn't take Ryan long to work that out. He holstered his gun, raced up the stairs and enveloped her in a hug, telling her she was safe, that everything was fine.

That kindness prompted the tears to really flow.

Ryan helped Buzz lift the new door from the delivery truck. The door Ryan had selected was strong and robust, much more secure than the old one and likely to withstand a barrage of bullets and kicks without giving way. Shane was inside the house, collecting the bullet casings for analysis, and Ryan desperately hoped that ballistics might give them a lead because his search of the area had yielded little more than some muddy footprints leading to the forest.

Buzz eyed the old door, in pieces on the deck. "What happened here?"

"Somebody tried to get in to the house," he said. "To hurt Kitty."

"Is she all right?"

"Yeah, she's fine for now."

Buzz pushed his baseball cap farther back on his head. "When I took your order over the phone, I had to tell my granddad I was delivering to someplace else."

"Why?"

"He says we're not to sell to Kitty anymore. He says we don't want her business."

"Well, you tell your granddad that this delivery is for me, because I live here now. I just became Kitty's new tenant."

Buzz seemed taken aback. "Granddad's not gonna like that."

"I kind of guessed he wouldn't."

Ryan motioned for Buzz to help him carry the door up the porch steps and onto the deck, where he leaned it against the outside wall.

"I can take it from here," he said, signing Buzz's delivery sheet. "Thanks for your help."

"No problem, sir."

Kitty came out onto the porch, carrying her cat under her arm. "Hey, Buzz," she said. "Does your granddad know you're here?"

"No, ma'am," he replied. "But when Chief Deputy Lawrence called in an emergency order, I just went and found the door you needed from our warehouse and brought it straight on down to you. I'm not really supposed to work this late."

Buzz puffed up his chest as if proud of himself for defying his grandfather's rules.

"I appreciate that," Kitty said with a warm smile. "Not many people around here would put themselves out for me."

"Maybe," Buzz said with a shrug. "But if we can't help a lady in need, then what's the town coming to?"

Ryan put a hand on Buzz's shoulder. That comment revealed maturity and a sense of decency in this young man.

"You're a good kid," he said, sliding a tip into his top pocket. "It's a shame that your granddad doesn't follow your lead."

Buzz nodded a shy farewell and made his way back to the truck.

"What's the story with the Price family?" Ryan asked Kitty. "What happened to Buzz's parents?"

"Buzz's dad is Tommy Price," Kitty replied. "Frank and Sheila's only son. He took off when

Buzz was in the first grade, leaving him with his parents." She looked skyward, appearing to be doing some mental calculation. "I haven't seen Tommy in about thirteen years now. Frank says he moved to Texas."

"What about Buzz's mother? What happened to her?"

"Elena was a girl from out of town, a drifter who sometimes stayed at a commune in the mountains and did casual work around Bethesda. After Buzz was born, she left pretty quick, giving Tommy parental responsibility. She never came back. It was a sad situation. I remember my mom offering to help out, but the Price family is proud. They didn't want anybody prying into their business."

"Well, I gotta say that someone's instilled good principles into that kid," Ryan said. "He's nothing like his grandfather."

"I think Frank's wife, Sheila, is the one to thank for Buzz's character. She's like a mom to him, but they're both bullied by Frank. He's a strong personality."

"He sure is," Ryan said. "He came marching into the station in a fit of temper this morning."

Kitty groaned, placing Shadow on the ground and leaning against the wall. "Let me guess—it was in response to my newspaper article."

"You've got it."

"Well, they needn't worry," she said. "That'll be the last one I write for the *Comanche Times* about my father."

Ryan was incredibly relieved. Perhaps Frank and Carla would be appeased by this news.

"Listen," he began, watching a swift swooping over the lake. "You've made some enemies in town by investigating a murder that's already been solved."

"It's not been solved," she said. "Because the wrong man is in prison."

He concentrated on tracking the swift, its undulating flight mesmerizing and calming. He would have to tread carefully with Kitty, not allowing his frustration to cause friction between them. But there were things she needed to hear.

"Kitty," he said, in what he hoped was a gentle, nonpatronizing tone. "Your dad had a lawyer who already did this kind of work for him. There was a police investigation and a full jury trial. If your father's lawyer couldn't generate reasonable doubt, what makes you so sure that you stand a better chance?"

"The court-appointed lawyer was useless," she replied, remembering how disappointed she had felt upon first meeting him. "He kept trying to persuade Dad to plead guilty and take a deal. He never believed in his innocence."

Ryan couldn't help but agree with the lawyer. "Taking a deal would probably have been a smart move."

"I know that you're not on my side in this," she said with obvious derision. "But I wish you'd keep your opinions to yourself. I don't need the negativity." She rubbed her temples. "This is hard enough already."

How hard did she think it was for the family of a murder victim? Kitty had no idea of the pain and suffering he had gone through, knowing his sister's last moments were likely filled with pain and fear. Just like the family of Molly Thomas, Ryan's family was also serving a life sentence, forever changed by that single devastating event. By denying that justice had been served for the Thomas family, Kitty was condemning Molly's parents to relive the murder over and over. It simply wasn't fair.

"I just want you to think about what you're doing," he said. "You're a young woman with your whole life ahead of you, and I don't want to see you waste it on a pointless fight."

She folded her arms across her chest and crinkled her brow. The Band-Aid on her forehead was beginning to peel at the edges and he resisted the urge to smooth it down with his thumbs.

"I'm not wasting my life," she said defensively. "I'm standing up for the truth, and even if it takes me fifty years, I will prove that my father didn't kill Molly."

Kitty's bullheadedness was maddening and Ryan felt he was fighting a losing battle. "Your investigation is putting you in danger," he said.

"I know that," she snapped. "Molly's real killer wants to eliminate me."

Ryan wondered if they might both be right. Kitty's attacker had clearly shown his willingness to kill. This went beyond someone just venting anger or aggravation at her—the man wanted her dead. Maybe he really was afraid that she'd uncover evidence against him. Not that Ryan thought Harry Linklater was innocent, but perhaps Harry had killed Molly with the help of an accomplice. That would certainly give someone a very big incentive to stop Kitty's investigation. Was Harry protecting the identity of a possible partner in crime? And was this person now determined to hide his involvement in the murder? It was a plausible line of inquiry, but Ryan knew he could never voice this theory to Kitty. She wouldn't accept any explanation that didn't fully clear her father.

"Whatever the motives of your attacker," he said, diplomatically, "you're in grave danger, so surely it makes sense to ease off the investigation until we catch this guy."

"No!" Did he just see a little stamp of her

foot? "I'll be going to see Harvey from the Starlight Bar tomorrow to question him about his witness testimony. I want to know why he lied. Every time I've tried to talk to him, he's shut me out, but I intend to make sure he acknowledges me this time."

"You can't harass someone like that," Ryan said in exasperation. "If Harvey doesn't want to speak with you, then you should leave him alone."

"For a law enforcement officer, you sure are closed-minded."

That comment stung. "I am not closed-minded," he said. "I'm able to see this situation from an impartial perspective."

"No, you're not," she retorted. "How can you be impartial when your sister was murdered just like Molly was? That fact will always affect your judgment."

He fell silent and Kitty did the same, a look of horror creeping across her face.

"I'm really sorry, Ryan," she said quietly. "I should never have brought up your sister, but I feel so strongly about my father's situation."

He was deeply disappointed that she had referenced his sister in the same sentence as her father. The names Gina Lawrence and Harry Linklater should never be placed side by side. One was an amazing girl cut down in childhood, and the other a convicted killer who should remain forever in a prison cell.

"We might need to learn to set some boundaries, huh?" Kitty said awkwardly. "Because we'll never see eye to eye on this."

"Right now, I'm more concerned with fixing this entrance and making you nice and secure," he said, heaving the door across the deck and into place. "I'll get on with this before I get an official statement from you. So in the meantime why don't you think about what happened today and jot down any details you can remember? We should build a profile of the guy and try to come up with a list of suspects."

"Sure, I'll leave you to it."

Ryan opened his toolbox and lifted out a screwdriver. He clenched the handle in his fingers, gripping tightly and letting the resentment flow out. Kitty had no clue how to set boundaries. She was incapable of seeing the truth, determined to win this battle at all costs, even her own life.

That short conversation had revealed a deep division between them, an insurmountable barrier that he had no idea how to bridge. Living here was going to be not only dangerous, but fraught with emotional difficulty.

THREE

Kitty awoke in darkness, certain that a bang had sounded outside. Reaching for her bedside lamp, she flicked the switch. Nothing. She had no idea of the time, but judging by her gritty eyes, she had been asleep for only two or three hours at most. She had taken an age to fall asleep the previous night and was exhausted, but adrenaline now flooded her tired body with energy. The power was out. Had her attacker caused it?

She pushed back the bedcovers and stood. The power in this old house had been known to fail oftentimes. Perhaps Ryan had inadvertently overloaded the circuit by plugging in one too many appliances. At least, that was what she hoped.

She reached for her robe in the moonlight, securing it tightly. She then picked up her gun from the dresser and approached her bedroom door with trepidation, hearing only the gentle swish of the trees outside.

She opened the door and stepped into the hall, to hear the slow ticking of her grandfather clock. The house was in perfect stillness, as if the furniture itself were sleeping. There was no sign of Ryan. Should she wake him? She wasn't sure. He had taken a statement from her the previous night, but it had been a difficult conversation, with tension still strong between them.

She heard a knocking sound below, coming from the cellar. The small underground room was dark and damp, accessed via a corner in the kitchen and used only for storing some of her father's old gardening equipment. She hadn't thought that the one tiny window down there was capable of accommodating an intruder, but perhaps she had been wrong. Creeping down the stairs, Kitty tried to step quietly, but each tiny squeak was amplified tenfold in the silence, ramping up her heart rate.

Once she reached the hallway, she approached Ryan's apartment door and knocked gently.

"Ryan," she called softly. "Are you awake?"

There was no reply. But the noises from the cellar grew louder, the sounds of items being moved, scraped across the floor.

"Ryan," she called, louder this time. "Somebody's here."

She tried the handle, finding the door unlocked. It opened onto his living room, dark and empty. She ventured inside, gun in hand.

"Hello?" she said, walking through his apartment and stopping at his open bedroom door. "It's me."

She poked her head around the door, seeing the bed crumpled and vacant. Ryan had gone. She turned to leave, fear settling deep down in the pit of her belly. Had somebody already got to him? Shadow meowed in the hallway, no doubt wondering if it was breakfast time already.

Moving back out into the house's main hallway and into the kitchen, she steadied herself, preparing to approach the cellar door. It was open, showing a staircase that descended into the pitch-black depths, cobwebby and grimy and terrifyingly creepy.

A bright beam from a flashlight shone in the darkness, falling on her face and hurting her eyes. Footsteps sounded on the bare steps, full and weighty, so she raised her gun, holding it as stable as she could.

"Kitty!" Ryan exclaimed, switching off the flashlight and activating the overhead light. "It's okay. I was just fixing the power. A fuse tripped during the night."

She lowered her gun, stepping back to sit heavily on a kitchen chair. Ryan came into the kitchen, closed the door behind him and brushed himself down. Wearing track pants and a sweat-shirt, he appeared younger than when he wore his uniform, his red hair tousled and endearing.

"A noise outside woke me up," he said. "I think somebody was in the barn."

"I heard a bang," she said. "Maybe it was the barn door blowing closed."

He went to the kitchen window to look out. "When I went to turn on the light in my room I realized there was no electricity. Does the power cut out here often?"

"Yes," she said. "Did you overload the circuit perhaps?"

"Um… I plugged in my radio charger last thing at night," he said, seemingly distracted by the view outside. "I think that might've been the cause."

"What do you see?" she asked.

"Someone's been here. It looks like white paint has been sprayed on the wall of the barn."

She joined Ryan at the window, squinting at the decrepit old building, dilapidated and dis-used for years now.

"I'll go out and take a look," Ryan said, turn-ing the key in the lock of the back door and slid-ing back the bolts he had added yesterday for extra security. "You stay here."

Without giving her time to argue, he slipped through the door and flitted across the yard, reaching the barn in a matter of seconds. Once there, he stopped and looked up at some white markings that were too far away for her to decipher. Then he went inside the barn itself, disappearing from view.

Opening a cupboard above her head, she rooted around for her mother's old bird-watching binoculars. Lifting them to her eyes, Kitty peered through the lenses at the barn while adjusting the focus. When the words sharpened into view, she didn't flinch or cry out in alarm. She simply sighed sadly and bowed her head in disappointment. In white paint, somebody had scrawled the message "Leave town!" They had even added an exclamation mark for dramatic effect.

By the time Ryan reentered the kitchen, she had filled the kettle and set it to boil, placing two cups on the counter in readiness.

"Would you like herbal tea?" she asked.

Ryan appeared confused. "Don't you want to know what I found?"

"I already know." She pointed to the binoculars. "I saw for myself."

"The barn padlock has been broken," he said, bolting the kitchen door behind him. "That was probably the bang you heard. Somebody used a ladder from inside to spray paint the words up high, but there's no sign of him now, unfortunately."

"It's just a stupid message," she said with a wave of her hand. "It doesn't matter."

She put fruit tea bags into the cups, humming to herself, pretending that this simply wasn't happening.

"Hey," Ryan said, rubbing her back, right between her shoulder blades. "It's okay to be upset by this. You don't have to try and be strong."

"Yes, I do, because if I crumble there's nobody to catch me. I'm all alone."

"I'm here," he said, failing to understand the emotional resonance she applied to the word *alone.* "I won't let anything happen to you. I've been thinking that your cellar would make an excellent panic room if you come under attack again. If I brick up the window, it'll be perfect. I'll get it set up for you if you like."

How had it come to this? Panic rooms were seen only in movies, not in sleepy Oklahoma towns.

"I guess it can't do any harm," she said.

"To be on the safe side, you shouldn't leave the house without informing me, at least until we catch this guy. I know it might sound extreme, but I'd rather I knew where you are at all times."

She nodded, too drained of energy to argue.

"In one way, we could view this incident as a

positive," he added. "It looks like your attacker is now focusing on running you out of town instead of hurting you."

"How do we know it's the same person?" she said. "This could be the work of somebody else entirely."

"It's probably the same guy. Maybe he saw that you're better protected now. Maybe he's scared of getting hurt. Or maybe he grew a conscience. Whatever the reason, it looks like he's backing off the aggressive tactics, and this has got to be good news, right?"

Kitty couldn't bring herself to share the same level of optimism. Ryan was reading far too much into this.

"It's a nice thought, Ryan," she said. "But my attacker is a murderer. He already killed Molly and won't stop until I'm dead, too." She gripped the edge of the counter with her fingers. "And the worst part is that if I'm dead, then nobody will fight for my dad in my place, because nobody believes me, not even you."

She felt her eyes grow sore with lack of sleep. She was so very tired of all this, of fearing for her life, of being alone in her terror day after day.

"I may not believe you, but I'm here for you," he said, turning her around and pulling her into his arms. "I can promise you that much."

She tried to fight the urge to give in to the comforting gesture, before succumbing and sliding her arms around his waist, resting her cheek on his chest. Ryan would never be the wholehearted supporter she wanted him to be, but she needed this affection from him so very much. The sensation of his firm arms around her torso was irresistible, providing a safe and stable place to relax and simply be.

For just a few moments, she let herself imagine that she wasn't entirely alone.

"Okay, let's all settle down," Ryan called out over the heads of at least seventy people packed into the Bethesda Town Hall. "Try and talk just one at a time."

The county sheriff rose from his chair on the stage and walked over to Ryan. Jim Wilkins was based in the main station at Lawton, rarely visiting the Bethesda satellite, so Ryan knew that the sheriff was taking this meeting seriously. He didn't like the bad publicity.

"I knew it was a bad idea for this town meeting to go ahead," Sheriff Wilkins said. "You should've refused to allow it."

"It's not within my authority to prevent the town from holding a meeting," Ryan replied, as the crowd murmured among themselves. "They're entitled to be here."

When Shane had informed Ryan of the emergency meeting, arranged by Frank Price to discuss Kitty Linklater, Ryan guessed that it was likely to deteriorate into anger and demands for retribution. And he had been correct. After just five minutes, there had been numerous calls for Kitty to be arrested, charged and imprisoned for everything from harassment to treason. It appeared that the community was deeply divided on this issue. Everyone seemed to agree that her father was guilty, but some residents defended Kitty's right to free speech, only to find that their pleas were often drowned out by the louder, more aggressive voices.

"I can handle it," Ryan assured his boss, a portly man in his sixties who was looking forward to retirement. "Why don't you take a seat with Shane?"

Then he turned to the crowd and shouted to gain their attention.

"Now listen up, everybody—I know feelings are running high. And I know you all love Molly's family and want to protect them from any more pain, but I need to remind you that we do things kindly here in Bethesda. Remain calm when you speak and think about what you're saying, because words can so easily turn cruel. Kitty's already come under physical attack and we should be mindful of her safety."

Frank was the first to stand, which came as no surprise to Ryan. The owner of the hardware store appeared to be Kitty's most vocal critic.

"If Kitty's gotten herself into hot water, then that's her own stupid fault. Her latest trick is the worst yet, and we're here to demand that something be done about it." He raised his hands in the air as if rallying his troops. "Isn't that right, folks?"

"Are you talking about the newspaper article?" Ryan asked. "Because Kitty has assured me it's the last piece she'll be writing in the paper about her father's murder conviction."

"No," Frank bellowed. "I'm not talking about the article. She did something much worse than that today. She actually went to Molly's grave, right in front of that poor child's family. Of all the dirty, low-down things she's done, this is the worst yet. She has no right to go there."

The murmurs and mutterings grew louder. Ryan heard words like *shameful* and *outrageous* in the hum.

"Can you tell me what happened?" he asked.

At this point, Nancy Buttaro stood. She was a friendly woman who ran the grocery store alongside her husband, Paul.

"It's the second anniversary of Molly's death today and Kitty went to the graveside to lay some flowers," Nancy said. "But Molly's parents turned up while she was there and got all upset. They asked Kitty to leave, which she did. No harm was done."

Ryan ran a hand down his face. Why would Kitty do such a thing? Not only had she riled up the town, but she'd failed to tell him that she was leaving the house. He'd spoken to her on the phone an hour ago and she hadn't mentioned a thing about this.

"Who are you to judge that no harm was done, Nancy?" Frank challenged. "Mrs. Thomas was traumatized to find a Linklater at her little girl's grave. It's plain wrong."

"Kitty promised me that she won't go there again," Nancy called back. "She came into the store right afterward and told me she regretted it. She was trying to be respectful toward Molly, but she messed up. Kitty's a decent young woman and she deserves to be left alone."

"She should leave Bethesda," Carla yelled, getting to her feet. "She's a nuisance, just like her drunken bum of a father."

"Now that's not fair," Nancy said, with a firm shake of her permed hair. "You should judge Kitty on her own actions, not those of her father."

"It sounds like you're on her side or something," Carla retorted. "Why don't you shut up and sit down, Nancy?"

Nancy's mouth dropped open in astonishment. "How dare you talk to me that way, Carla. Why can't we just be nicer to one another? And why are we having this public meeting, anyway? Aren't we meant to be trying to protect the Thomas family from more hurt and pain?" She looked around the room. "Us folks fighting like schoolkids sure isn't gonna help."

"Looks like I was right about you," Carla yelled. "You *are* on her side."

Within seconds, the meeting had descended into chaos yet again as insults and accusations flew, forcing Ryan to bang the table with his fist.

"Calm down," he called. "This isn't getting us anywhere."

"Look what she's doing to the community," Frank yelled over the ruckus. "Can't you do something about her?"

Ryan waited for the noise to die down. "I'm not sure what you expect me to do, Frank. Kitty hasn't broken the law and she's just trying to do what's right for her father. And all it's gotten her is verbal attacks and physical assault. Don't you feel at least a little sympathy for her?"

Frank's reply was emphatic. "No, I don't."

"Well, maybe you could try harder to find some compassion. She's been through a lot."

"Can I ask you something, sir?" Frank said, resuming his seat next to Sheila, whose eyes were downcast and submissive. "Do you think Harry Linklater is guilty?"

"Yes," Ryan replied firmly. "Yes, I do. And in my opinion, he should never be released from prison after what he did."

That's when he saw her, standing at the back of the hall, shrinking into the corner, unnoticed by all except him. Kitty's expression was one of hurt as she watched the proceedings, as she heard him say that he hoped her father would be incarcerated forever. But he had spoken the truth. He couldn't change the way he felt, nor did he want to.

"Well, at least you're smart enough to see that," Frank grumbled. "But her father's locked away where he can't hurt anyone—Kitty's the one hurting the town now. She's been harassing Harvey Flynn from the Starlight Bar again today, accusing him of lying to the police and of deliberately destroying his CCTV footage from the night of the murder. Now surely that kind of pestering behavior is illegal?"

Ryan tore his gaze from Kitty and scanned the room for Harvey, whom he had met just once when doing an introductory tour of the town's establishments. He finally found the tall bearded man standing at the side of the hall.

"Do you wish to make a complaint against Kitty, Mr. Flynn?" Ryan asked.

Harvey shook his head and held up a hand in a dismissive gesture, which clearly was not the action that some of the crowd had been hoping for.

Carla stood up again. "Harvey's just being nice because Kitty's a woman all on her own and he doesn't want to see her get into any trouble."

"Except she's not all on her own," Frank said with a sneer. "She's got a man staying in the apartment."

Ryan closed his eyes, knowing exactly where this was heading. It wasn't that he minded the residents knowing of his living arrangements, but he wanted to tell everyone on his own terms. It didn't take long for Frank to ruin those plans, as he turned his back on Ryan to address the crowd.

"Chief Deputy Lawrence is Kitty Linklater's newest tenant, folks. And he's been fixing up her house with new doors and all sorts of other things, so none of us need to feel sorry for her. She's got herself her very own bodyguard, which is more than Molly Thomas ever had."

Howls of protest could be heard, but Carla seemed to be particularly incensed by this piece of news. "How could you, Deputy Lawrence?" she challenged. "How could you pay rent to the daughter of a murderer?"

Ryan pinched the bridge of his nose with his thumb and forefinger, noticing Sheriff Wilkins covering his horrified face with his hands. Meanwhile, Frank leaned back in his chair with a satisfied smile.

"Kitty's in danger," Ryan shouted. "She needs protection and I need a place to live, so it makes good sense for me to be there." He caught her eye. "But I'm not supporting her campaign to free her father. I want to make that clear."

"Shame on you," Carla yelled, pointing a finger. "You should be putting your efforts into serving the community, not lining the pockets of Kitty Linklater."

At this moment, Joe stood up beside his wife. "What can we do to help? If Kitty's in danger, then who knows which one of us could be next."

Carla rolled her eyes. Clearly, this was a bone of contention between the two of them, but Ryan was glad of the show of support toward the interests of law and order.

"You can keep your eyes and ears open," Ryan said. "Look out for anyone acting suspiciously or asking a lot of questions about Kitty. As a community, we can keep everyone safe if we pull together."

Despite murmurs of agreement in the crowd, Carla did not seem appeased. "If Kitty took more responsibility for her actions, then I'm sure she wouldn't be facing any danger." She turned to the town's bar owner. "I hope you'll make a complaint to the sheriff about Kitty harassing you, Harvey, because I don't think our new chief deputy intends on doing anything about her awful behavior."

While Harvey again made a dismissive gesture, Sheriff Wilkins stood and approached Ryan, saying quietly into his ear, "I want a word with you later about your living arrangements here in Bethesda."

Ryan sighed. This was not going to plan at all. Then Kitty's voice rang out across the hall, far louder than he'd thought her capable of.

"The real reason Harvey doesn't want to make a complaint about me is because he lied in court about the night of Molly's murder," she said. "And he doesn't want the police asking any awkward questions."

She was walking down the middle aisle, between the rows of chairs, hair piled high in a messy bun, tendrils falling on her face. She had made a little more effort with her clothes that day, wearing tailored pants and a blouse.

"Perhaps now isn't the best time to be doing this, Kitty," Ryan said, jumping from the stage and approaching her. "Tensions are running too high."

She ignored his advice, as he'd suspected she would.

"Your CCTV footage from that night wasn't lost, was it, Harvey? You deliberately destroyed it."

A hush fell as numerous people looked from Kitty to the barman and back, clearly shocked at this sudden showdown.

"That's not true," Harvey said. "I wish you'd drop all this nonsense, Kitty."

She stopped in her tracks and stared him down. "There was another man who arrived at the bar just after midnight, wasn't there? He got there soon after Molly's death. I received a call from my newest witness today. He says he remembered something else about that night which might be relevant. He claims you let a man in the back door and there was an argument between the two of you in the corridor. You told the guys in the bar that it was an old friend looking for a place to stay. So I want to know who he was and why you didn't tell the police about him."

Harvey stepped forward. "I saw the article about your witness in the newspaper. I remember him coming into the bar and drinking whiskey until he passed out. He's a drunk just like your father, nothing but a deadbeat drunk who probably can't remember what he ate for breakfast this morning let alone what he saw and heard a couple of years ago."

Kitty cheeks reddened. "Having an alcohol addiction doesn't make him a deadbeat."

"Oh, come on, Kitty," Harvey said angrily. "Stop kidding yourself that your dad's a good guy. He served eight years in prison."

"That was a long time ago. He's changed."

"Guys like that don't change. Once a felon, always a felon."

"No," she shouted. "You don't really know him."

Harvey laughed, but it seemed forced. "I know that he never loved you as much as he loved the booze. His brain was fried by it."

Kitty's face seemed to break, beginning with her brows, then moving to her eyes, cheeks and mouth. Ryan put a hand on her forearm.

"I'll take you home," he said.

She pushed him away and pointed at Harvey.

"*You're* the one who kept feeding Dad alcohol and taking his money," she shouted in the quiet hall. "You knew that my mom's death destroyed him and you used his grief to increase your profits. Your bar was practically his second home for ten years." A tear fell, and she quickly brushed it away. "The only thing wrong with my father's brain is that it told him you were a friend, when you were only ever his enemy. If anyone here deserves to feel shame, it's you, Harvey."

A few gasps were audible in the silence and

Harvey stood immobile, hands thrust into his pockets. From the looks of it, the truths she told him had hit home. He hung his head.

"I recently decided to close the bar and start over somewhere else," he said. "I hope that helps bring everybody in Bethesda some closure."

"No," she retorted. "Closure only happens when you start telling the truth about the night of the murder."

Harvey shrugged his shoulders, shook his head and walked to the exit. Kitty watched him leave, breathing hard, nostrils flaring. Ryan studied her in reluctant admiration. Despite her being wrong on this matter, she fought her case with passion and pride, refusing to bow to the criticism of the crowd. She stood alone and yet she stood tall. He felt an unwelcome attraction to her beginning to develop. That was the last thing he needed.

"Okay, folks," he called out. "The show's over. Let's all go home and calm down, and if you have any information, come see me at the station." He looked at Frank as he added, "No more public meetings about this, okay?"

Ryan then steered Kitty to a nearby vacant chair and encouraged her to sit, which she did, leaning forward and putting her head in her hands.

"I just wanted to lay flowers on Molly's

grave," she said. "I miss her, too." She took the clip from her hair and allowed the loose strands to cascade down her shoulders. "I used to babysit for her when she was little, and we had a strong bond. I intended to be really quick at the graveside so that no one would notice me. The last thing I wanted was to upset her parents. It was a bad idea."

Ryan crouched at her side, one knee on the floor, as the hall emptied. "It was a terrible idea, Kitty, not least because you put yourself in harm's way. I thought we'd agreed that you wouldn't leave the house without telling me where you're headed."

"Like my very own bodyguard," she said, imitating Frank's mocking tone. "I don't want to be tied to someone who openly wants my dad to spend the rest of his life in prison."

He couldn't deny his deep disgust for her father and his crime. Harry didn't deserve to breathe free air again for the rest of his life.

"I'm sorry," he said. "I can't help how I feel."

"And I can't help how I feel, either. I needed to leave the house to follow up my new lead."

"You mean the phone call from your witness?"

"He said he remembered Harvey arguing with a man late that night," she said. "Harvey deliberately covered it up."

Ryan didn't quite know how to say this, so he

just came out with it. "A man with an alcohol dependency isn't likely to accurately remember what happened two years ago. His testimony is too unreliable for you to get excited about it."

A deliberate cough sounded in his vicinity and Ryan looked up to see Sheriff Wilkins standing over him, thumbs hooked into his belt loops.

"Sorry to break up this little party," the sheriff said with obvious disapproval. "But can I have a word with you now, Ryan?"

"Sure," he said, rising and whispering to Kitty, "I'll only be a few minutes, so don't go anywhere, okay?"

She nodded her understanding.

Sheriff Wilkins led him to the side of the hall, his expression stern. "What's this about you living down at the Linklater house?"

"I rent an apartment there," he explained. "It's no big deal."

"Of course it's a big deal," the sheriff retorted. "You know I'm retiring soon and I think you'd make a perfect replacement, but how do you think the folks of this county will feel when they hear you're cavorting with the daughter of a convicted killer?"

"I'm not *cavorting* with her, Jim. She's in danger down there. She needs my help."

"And she'll get all the help she needs from the sheriff's department when she calls to report an attack, just like anyone else. We'll all look after her, Ryan. But you can't afford to be personally associated with her, and if you don't put a stop to this little friendship you can kiss my endorsement goodbye come election time. You can start by finding yourself another place to live. Do I make myself clear?"

Ryan rubbed his forehead. This had to be one of the worst days in his career.

"Yes, sir. You're perfectly clear."

"Good."

He stalked off toward Shane, adjusting his hat as he went, leaving Ryan to consider his predicament. As much as he didn't want to ruin his reputation in town—and his chance at becoming sheriff—this could be a matter of life-and-death for Kitty. He couldn't simply abandon her, no matter what anyone said.

He turned around, only to see Kitty's chair empty.

"Oh, Kitty," he muttered under his breath. "Can't you stay still for five minutes?"

He walked to the back of the empty hall and opened the door. He saw people returning to their cars and homes, no doubt discussing the high drama they'd witnessed, but he did not see Kitty. Then he heard a scream, a shrill and penetrating shriek that caused his anxiety to surge.

The scream had come from the woods.

FOUR

Kitty's scream died away as a hand once again clamped over her mouth.

She had never intended to put herself in harm's way, but she'd been careless. She'd wanted to leave the stifling hall, simmering hot with the righteous anger of the town, and escape into the night air, where a light and cool rain had begun to fall. And with all the people around her, she had assumed she would be safe to wait for Ryan while sitting inside her car. How wrong she had been.

She had stupidly parked her car in the far corner of the lot, an unlit and secluded place—a decision that no doubt reflected her sense of seclusion in Bethesda. Once she had reached her vehicle and delved into her pocket for the key, a man had sprung from behind her, dragging her quickly and silently into the dense woodland opposite the town hall. His hand across her mouth meant she could only squeal and struggle futilely. Thankfully, a swift elbow to his stomach allowed her to gain a second or two to let out a yell of alarm.

She was dragged past tree after tree, her heels digging into the soil and turning up the earth. She clawed at passing branches, but they slid through her fingers, leaving her with nothing but handfuls of soggy leaves. Her attacker's arms were thin, but sinewy and muscled, and she felt them tense beneath his baggy sweatshirt as he finally pressed her, face forward, to the trunk of a nearby tree. She turned her head to the side, breathing heavily through her nose, her lips pinched and bruised beneath his tight fingers.

Then a knife glinted in the dying light, inches from her face. It was covered in tiny water droplets clinging to the steel from the misty rain that was falling. Kitty reacted instantly, bucking like a horse, determined that the blade would not touch her skin, but she could only flinch in horror as she felt its sharp edge against her cheek. A stinging sensation made her shiver as blood trickled down onto her neck, into the collar of her blouse. Although she could not see the man's face, she sensed his enjoyment at the sight of her blood.

Someone was shouting her name close by. Her attacker heard it, too, and responded by moving the knife to his side and dragging her around the tree, its huge trunk concealing them from view. He pinned her against the bark, his hand forced down so heavily on her mouth that she grew light-headed. His masked face was millimeters from hers, his eyes barely visible through the tiniest of slits. He was perfectly still, waiting, the knife poised at her throat.

Kitty saw Ryan run straight past, gun in hand, heading farther into the woods to search for her. She wanted to shout, but could only murmur. As she watched him continue, her belly flipped over. Soon he would be out of sight and she would be alone with a murderous man, under the blade of his knife.

Once Ryan was far enough away, she felt sure this cruel man would dispatch her quickly and disappear into the woods. The seconds were ticking by, and Ryan's figure was rapidly being swallowed by the mist. She had to do something, make a noise or movement, anything to catch his attention—without spooking her attacker into slitting her throat. Slowly, surreptitiously, she reached into her jacket pocket and pulled out her keys, which had a flashlight key ring. After pressing the button, she shook the keys in her hand, sending the beam of light dancing among the trees.

Ryan stopped, obviously noticing the glimmer. When he turned and began to run back,

Kitty sagged with relief. Her assailant pulled away from her and she dropped to her knees, her legs suddenly unable to take her full weight. As she panted in the dirt, catching her breath, Ryan pounded past in pursuit of the masked man. Kitty could only watch as Ryan leaped in the air, coming down on the running figure, grappling him to the ground, where they began to scuffle, rolling over in the wet leaves.

More voices echoed among the trees and numerous footsteps could be heard running their way. Kitty recognized the voices of Carla and Joe from the restaurant, Nancy and Paul from the grocery store.

Nancy appeared in her line of sight and called out, "We heard a scream. Is that you, Kitty?"

"Go back," shouted Ryan, as he wrestled with the masked man. "Get out of here."

More townspeople appeared and they watched the commotion, eyes wide. Paul and Nancy approached Kitty, helping her to her feet, brushing her down.

"Ryan wants us to go," Kitty panted. "It's dangerous."

"Shouldn't we help?" Paul asked. "There's only one of him but a bunch of us."

This comment seemed to fire up Joe, who pushed up his sleeves and said, "Whoever this guy is, he picked on the wrong town."

With that, he rushed forward, closely followed by a few other male onlookers. As they approached the fighting men, Ryan called, "No!" But Joe made an attempt to grab Kitty's attacker by his shirt.

Joe's effort to assist backfired, as his intervention caused Ryan to loosen his grasp, allowing the man to jump to his feet and pull a gun from an inside pocket. Holding his weapon in the air, he fired a shot that reverberated through the woods. Everybody screamed and dropped to the ground, except Ryan, who pulled his weapon out in response, aiming at the assailant.

They stood only yards apart, guns pointed at each other, a standoff that she could only pray would go Ryan's way.

Ryan stared down the barrel of a gun, breathing hard, his protective instincts in overdrive. There must be at least eight townsfolk behind him, including Kitty, and they were in severe danger.

"Slowly put down your weapon and raise your hands in the air," Ryan said. "Let's end this right here."

The man responded by taking a firm step forward and pointing his gun directly at Kitty's head. She squeezed her eyes tightly shut and the unarmed people nearby let out whimpers of alarm.

"If you take a shot, I'll kill you," Ryan warned, realizing that a different approach was needed here. This man wouldn't surrender; if Ryan forced the issue, it would turn into a gunfight. "Be coolheaded and nobody gets hurt. Back away slowly."

Under the circumstances, Ryan had no choice but to let the guy go. As the people cowered on the ground behind him, he called out reassuringly, "Don't worry, folks. Keep calm and this will be over soon."

He watched with seething hostility as the suspect began to take small steps backward, never lowering his gun, facing forward until he had put a fair distance between them. Then he turned and ran. For a split second Ryan considered giving chase, before coming to his senses. His priority was to safeguard those around him.

He turned to Kitty and saw her standing, flanked by Nancy and Paul, blood on one cheek, a deep red stain soaked into the collar of her blouse.

"You're hurt," he said, reaching into his pocket for a clean tissue.

She took the tissue from his hand. "It's just a scratch. It could've been a lot worse."

How on earth could Ryan even consider severing his living arrangement with Kitty now? If she hadn't managed to scream out, she could be dead by now. Similarly, if he wasn't at her house when this guy came back, she'd be totally exposed. Calling 9-1-1 might not get help to her fast enough.

"Who was that?" Nancy asked, looking anxiously through the trees. "And what was he doing here?"

Kitty provided an answer before Ryan could speak. "That was the man who killed Molly, and now he's trying to kill me, too."

Carla clicked her tongue in annoyance, having not lost any of the feistiness she'd shown in the town hall. "Don't talk nonsense, Kitty. Your father killed Molly and that awful man wants to hurt you because you refuse to believe it."

"Let's not speculate about why Kitty is being attacked," Ryan said. "What's important is that we pull together to make sure Bethesda remains a safe place for all of us. I'll be writing a report about this incident, so I'd like as many eyewitness accounts as possible."

Nancy raised her hand. "Paul and I would be glad to help."

"Thank you. I'll take your statements when you're ready."

"I hope your report will show that Kitty put

the whole town in danger," Carla said. "That man could've hurt any of us."

"We can't blame Kitty for that," Ryan said.

"Can't we?" Carla retorted. She was clearly shaken by what had just happened. "She's been telling lies for too long and now she's got someone angry enough to lash out." She pressed a palm to her chest. "I thought I was going to die."

"A violent man like this is a danger to all of us, honey," Joe said, patting his wife's shoulder reassuringly. "He's mad at Kitty today, but who knows what might set him off next? We should do what we can to help the investigation instead of creating more division."

"I'm not the one creating division here." Carla folded her arms defiantly. "Next time something like this happens, I won't come running and put myself in the line of fire."

Ryan clenched his jaw in irritation. Yes, Kitty was wrong to have visited Molly's grave. Yes, she was mistakenly loyal to her father. And yes, she had stupidly put herself in danger by going outside alone. But she didn't deserve this, not by a long shot.

"I know you'll all be keen to get home so I'll be available to take statements at the station from eight o'clock tomorrow morning," he said to the small crowd of people. "I'd appreciate seeing as many of you as possible. If you'd like to make your way toward the parking lot now, I'll bring up the rear and have your backs, okay?"

Kitty tugged on his sleeve, pointing to a spot on the ground.

"The guy dropped his knife in the fight," she said. "It's what he used to cut my face."

Ryan pulled an evidence bag from his pocket and carefully picked up the blade from the leaves. There wouldn't be any prints, given the gloves the man had worn, and the chances of finding anything that would lead back to the knife's owner on this commonly sold kitchen knife were slim, but finding any leads in this case would be like finding gold.

"Let's go," he said, putting an arm around Kitty.

She held the tissue against her cheek as she walked, occasionally moving it to check if the bleeding had stemmed. The wound wasn't large or deep enough to require stitches, but it might still leave a faint scar once healed. At the moment he guessed that a skin blemish was the least of her worries.

"You shouldn't have left the town hall without me," he said. "It was reckless."

"Yes, it was," she admitted. "I'm sorry—I just don't seem to be able to do anything right today." She sighed. "It's hard to stay positive when so many people hate me."

"I don't hate you." His feelings were complicated, far too muddled to explain. "I really don't."

"I'm not sure I believe you," she said. "Sometimes I think you don't like me very much at all." She lowered her head. "And I'm not sure I like you much, either."

His heart sank.

"Don't get me wrong," she continued. "I'm really grateful for everything you're doing to help me, but your hostility toward my father constantly hangs over us." Her eyes welled up. "I trust my father with all my heart and even though you've never met him, you write him off like he's devious and wicked."

Ryan fixed his line of sight on the parking lot ahead, lit up brightly in the darkness. How could he tell Kitty that her father most likely *was* devious and wicked? How could he lead her to the horrible truth that child killers were, by their very nature, devoid of morals? He could say none of this. It wouldn't help matters at all.

"Listen to me," he said. "You've got me all wrong. I like you very much, and I hope you can learn to like me. We could even be friends. But I have to remind you that you're putting yourself in unnecessary danger by fighting to free your father. You saw how angry some of the people were tonight. Not just your attacker—the people in the meeting, too. They want you to stop. *I* want you to stop."

She stopped dead in her tracks. "I don't care what you want. I'll do this with or without you, and no amount of town meetings or petitions or even violent attacks will stop me."

Up ahead, the townsfolk had reached the lot and were speaking to Sheriff Wilkins, animatedly recounting the scene they had witnessed in the woods. Ryan heard the sheriff call his name.

"We're okay, Sheriff," he yelled back. "I'll be right there."

He then lightly gripped Kitty by the shoulders. "Petitions and nasty comments can't kill you, but knives and guns can. That guy might have been in the town hall tonight, getting all riled up. He might be someone that you know, someone that you've passed on the street regularly, just waiting for the right moment to strike. This man is obviously depraved and you're giving him a reason to target you."

"So you think I should just stop what I'm doing, huh?" She shrugged her shoulders, dislodging his hands. "You think I should let a killer stay on the loose, free to murder again."

"I think you should leave the investigation to the professionals," he said. "We could be dealing with an accomplice here—"

She cut him off by raising a palm. "What

did you say? Do you think that my father had an accomplice?"

Ryan groaned inwardly. He should never have said those words out loud. He tried to backtrack. "It's just a theory at the moment."

She was simmering with indignation. "Well, it's the stupidest theory I've ever heard."

He bristled at being called stupid. He was far wiser than she was in this matter.

"I have to consider every plausible explanation for these attacks on you," he said, raising his voice and letting his irritation show. "And I rely on facts, not fantasy. You need to learn to tell fantasy from reality, because right now you don't seem to know the difference."

Kitty raised her voice to match his. "Oh, I know the difference, all right. I know you have a fantasy that we'll be friends, but reality is proving far different."

Ryan turned and threw his hands up in the air, with no clue of what else to say.

Just then Sheriff Wilkins approached them through the trees. "I heard a gunshot," he said. "And I've been told there was an incident."

"Kitty was attacked again," Ryan said. "The guy escaped, but I'll be writing a report tomorrow morning and issuing alerts right away to try and apprehend him."

Sheriff Wilkins eyed the cut on Kitty's cheek.

"I can see you're bleeding. Do you need to go to the hospital?"

"It's not serious," she replied. "I can see to it with my first aid kit. I really want to go home now."

"Of course you do," the sheriff said. "Only I heard raised voices just now, like you two were having an argument."

"It's nothing," Ryan said.

The sheriff looked between the two of them. "I wondered if Ryan's decision regarding renting your apartment had caused some friction, Miss Linklater. But you should know it's for the best."

Ryan shot the sheriff a warning look. "Kitty's upset about the attack and she got a little agitated. We're not fighting. I'll take her home now, if I may. Could you supervise the lot and ensure everyone leaves safely?"

"I'd be happy to help," the sheriff replied. "It's been a traumatizing evening for everyone and we need to keep tensions from flaring." He tipped his hat to Kitty. "I'll leave you in Ryan's capable hands, ma'am, and please rest assured that we'll thoroughly investigate what happened here."

When the sheriff was out of earshot, Kitty said, "I'm sorry I raised my voice. You didn't deserve the things I said, especially after you came to save me." She held out a hand as a peace offering. "Can we forget it?"

He took her hand. It was cool and stiff. Her touch was oddly formal, standoffish and awkward. Ryan sensed that she wasn't really calling a truce. She was simply delaying the next disagreement.

"I'm sorry, too," he said. "I forget how hard this is for you."

"Why did the sheriff mention you renting the apartment?" she asked. "What did he mean when he said it's for the best?"

"He's confused," Ryan replied. "I think he mixed me up with one of his other deputies."

Kitty didn't look convinced. "Does he have an issue with you living at my house?"

Now would be the perfect time to tell her that he had been ordered to vacate her apartment. But there was no way he could leave her now, not while she was being hunted. He would have to take the consequences.

"The sheriff's opinion doesn't matter to me. It's my business and nobody else's."

As he saw her safely into her car, ready to escort her home, he couldn't quite believe that he was potentially sacrificing his dream job for the sake of a woman who was loyal to a murderer.

But what choice did he have? She wouldn't last five minutes without him.

* * *

Kitty handed Ryan a glass of iced tea as he packed away his tools. For the last few hours, he had been installing a panic alarm in her cellar and fitting a new heavy-duty door, delivered that morning from a store in Lawton. Kitty had initially insisted on paying for it, but when she heard the price, the horror she'd felt must have shown on her face. So Ryan had offered to pay for it in lieu of two weeks' rent and she had accepted the offer, glad she didn't have to rely on his charity.

They both stood in the small cellar as Ryan drained his glass. The space was cramped and claustrophobic, but Ryan had pushed her father's old machinery to the side to make a little more room to move. Now that he had bricked up the small, high window, the cellar felt like a dungeon—dark and gloomy. Kitty kept telling herself that this room was for emergencies only, because even as she stood there, perfectly safe with Ryan, she fought the urge to run up to the kitchen and surround herself with sunshine and fresh air.

"So this is the button you press if you're in danger," Ryan said, pointing to a device he had attached to the wall, with wires trailing into the circuit box above. "It links directly to my emergency radio so I'll hear the alarm wherever I am."

He pressed the button and within a second or two a high-pitched beep sounded in the radio on his belt. It made her think of a war siren, an alarm that signaled the approach of devastating danger and imminent loss of life, something she'd once seen in a movie. She leaned against the wall, suddenly light-headed, feeling the chill of the brick seep through her sweater.

Ryan looked up the stairs. "That new door is strong enough to hold for a good while, so it should buy you enough time. If the telephone line is cut then the button won't work, so keep your gun and cell with you at all times as an extra precaution. You can't afford to take any chances."

She put a palm on her forehead. The scene he was conjuring up was terrifying. She imagined being alone in this cold, dark space, hearing shots being fired into a door that might or might not hold until Ryan reached her. Could she defend herself with just her handgun? Would she have the confidence and cool head to point her weapon and fire at an intruder?

"Hey," Ryan said, gazing at her face. "You've gone really pale." He directed her toward the stairs. "Let's get you out of here."

She climbed the steps into her welcoming,

bright kitchen and sat at the table, gathering her thoughts and placing her head in her hands.

"I know this is a lot to take in," Ryan said, closing the door to the cellar. "But you have to be prepared for the worst."

"I hate living this way," she said. "I just wish I knew who was doing this to me."

He sat opposite her. "We're working really hard on finding that out. I received an email report this morning on the bullet casings, so we know which gun he used, and I've got Shane going house to house with the profile we built of him." He put his hands in the air, acknowledging her resigned expression. "I know we don't have much to work with, because he's taken care to cover himself and wear gloves, but you've helped a lot by telling me everything you can remember."

"I'm sure I wasn't much help at all," she conceded. "I could barely recall a thing."

"That's normal in victims of assault," he said, putting his fingers on top of hers. "But I also got five witness reports from those folks who came into the woods yesterday. So far, we know that we're looking for an average-height man with a slender build who owns a Glock G19 handgun."

She smiled weakly. "It's not much to go on, huh?"

"It's a start."

"Thank you for everything," she said. "You're working hard on keeping me safe and I appreciate it."

"No problem."

A silence ensued as Kitty gazed out the window, watching a noisy flock of ducks flying toward the lake. When she was a kid, she used to spend her entire summers swimming or boating at Whistling Lake. She'd stay there until dusk, until she heard her mother calling, reminding her that bedtimes were enforced even in the summer months. Back then her dad had been sober, running a thriving gardening business. Kitty's home had once been a place of joy and love and contentment. Now it had become her prison.

"Is something bothering you, Kitty?" Ryan asked. "I mean something other than the obvious."

"I miss my mom," she blurted out. "I wish she was here now, taking charge, telling me it's all gonna be okay."

He leaned over the table. "It's all gonna be okay."

His attempt to comfort her in her grief fell flat and only compounded her sense of loneliness. Her mother would listen to her, would trust Kitty's instincts, believe in her. Ryan did none of those things.

"I'm not very good at being a counselor, am I?" he said with a half laugh. "Why don't you tell me about your mom? I'd like to know more about her."

Kitty didn't know where to start. Her mother was a force of nature, wonderful and vibrant, with so many differing sides to her personality.

"When I was a little girl I used to tell my friends that my mom was a beauty queen, because she always wore a pretty dress and styled her hair each morning. Even when the cancer treatment took its toll, she never let herself go. After she lost her hair she bought a beautiful dark wig and still put on makeup every day. She never gave up. Never." Kitty smiled. "So maybe you can see where I get my determined streak from."

Ryan nodded. "I'm sure she'd be proud of the woman you've become."

"I hope so," she said. "I never expected to lose her so young and it was made all the worse when my dad fell apart. When you're happy you don't think the good times will end, so you take them for granted." She gingerly touched the cut on her cheek. "When you're happy you have no idea that everything can change in an instant."

"I understand what you're saying," Ryan said. "When Gina died, a weight fell across our family. It's like there's a before time and an after time, a line drawn right down the middle of our lives, separating the two halves. One half is full of life and the other half is full of…"

He seemed to struggle to find the right word, so she helped him out. "Darkness?"

"Yeah, a lot like darkness, where you don't know which way to turn or how to find your way back to happiness."

She stared earnestly at his face. "I know exactly what you mean."

"The before time ends up feeling a little like a dream," he continued. "You start forgetting small details, like what a person smelled like or what their laugh sounded like. Grief can catch you off guard when you least expect it, like when you see a kid riding a bicycle with a pink basket."

She found herself listening to him intently. So she and Ryan did have something in common, after all. He was able to articulate her feelings better than she ever could, clearly able to understand how she felt about losing her mother at much too young an age.

"Do you think it's possible?" she asked.

"What?"

"To find your way back to happiness. Do you think it's possible?"

"I do," he said. "'And the light shineth in darkness; and the darkness comprehended it not.'"

She took a quick, deep breath, blinking away her emotion. It had been many months since a verse of Scripture had lifted her from the depths of despair. In fact, it had been many months since she'd attended church. Ryan had quoted more than words—he had reminded her that light existed, that she was loved even in her loneliness, *especially* in her loneliness.

"You will be happy again, Kitty," he said, taking her hand and twining his fingers through hers. "Our lowest points are always the start of something new and incredible."

Could she possibly allow herself to believe that? She'd assumed that by the age of twenty-nine she'd be married and settled, perhaps with a family and a busy, wonderfully hectic life. Instead, she'd been at her lowest point for ten years, ever since her mom died and her dad started drinking. How much longer did she have to wait for the start of something better? Kitty often wondered if she had experienced the worst of her anguish or if there was more to come. Surely it couldn't get worse than this?

"Don't give up," he said, squeezing her fingers. "One day you'll look back on this point of your life as a time of character building. You'll be a better person because of all your bad experiences, Kitty. I know it."

She smiled, enjoying the sensation of his hand

in hers, for the first time feeling truly at ease in his presence, valuing his company as if he truly were a friend and she could tell him anything.

"You know something, Ryan?" she said. "What you said earlier was wrong—I think you *are* a pretty good counselor."

He laughed. "Well, I'll sure take that compliment from you, especially as it's such a rare occurrence."

"I don't mean to be so difficult and tetchy all the time," she said. "It's just that..." She stopped. "You know why."

"I know why."

And then the sensation of calm left her, almost as quickly as it had come, replaced with the knowledge that however much Ryan could empathize with her pain, he would never believe her. He wouldn't stand with her when it truly mattered, when her father's reputation was at stake. She would therefore need to be careful to keep him at arm's length and avoid these kinds of intimate discussions. They were destined to lead nowhere good.

She pulled her hand free and stood up. "Okay, let's go through the panic room procedure one more time. I want to be totally clear how to protect myself from whatever's coming my way."

FIVE

Kitty made breakfast in the morning, listening to Ryan moving around the apartment, his radio occasionally crackling to life. Even though it had been a quiet night, she was comforted by these sounds of normal life.

"Hey," he said, stepping out into the hall in a crisply ironed uniform. "You're up early."

"I didn't sleep well, so I got up before sunrise. I just made toast and coffee if you want some."

"Thanks. It's good to have an uneventful night, huh?" He came into the kitchen and poured himself a cup of coffee. "You didn't hear anything, did you?"

"No. All quiet."

"So what are your plans today?" he asked, sitting down and buttering some toast.

"This morning I'll be writing an article for a women's magazine about how to declutter your home." She grimaced. "It's not the kind of work I'd normally do, but it pays the bills." She sat at the table. "Unfortunately, my reputation as a serious journalist took a hit after my articles for the *Comanche Times* went out. None of the respectable Oklahoma papers seem to want my services anymore. They're worried I'll try and use them to publish more articles about my father."

"It'll pick up," he said. "Just you wait and see."

"Hmm," she said. "I'm not so sure. I got an email from the editor of the *Comanche Times* this morning asking me to take a sabbatical. They want to let the heat die down before I submit another piece."

"Well, when you've finished your article for the women's magazine, let me take a look." He smiled. "I could use some advice on how to declutter."

She drew a circle with her fingernail on the kitchen table, wanting to raise an issue but knowing that Ryan was likely to have a problem with it. "After I write the article, I'd hoped to go and visit my dad."

"You can't drive to the Oklahoma State Penitentiary by yourself," Ryan said. "Does it have to be today?"

Kitty hadn't seen her father in over a week. She was his only visitor, his only source of contact with the outside world, and he would be missing her.

"I really wanted to go today," she said. "He always expects me on Thursdays."

"Can you delay it until tomorrow instead? And I'll be able to accompany you."

"You can't make it this afternoon?"

"I've taken a lot of time off since I started working in Bethesda, so I should put in a full day today." He raised his eyebrows. "Sheriff Wilkins might start asking questions if he gets wind of it."

Ryan had delivered that last comment with a smile, but she sensed a slight antagonism toward the sheriff. He and Ryan had exchanged heated words at the town hall and the aftermath was clearly lingering. Perhaps the sheriff had taken exception to the time his chief deputy was devoting to dealing with her situation.

"Okay," she said, not wanting to put him out any more than she had already. "We'll go tomorrow instead. I'll call the prison today and give them advance notice."

"Great." He reached for his hat on the chair next to him. "Remember to keep yourself locked in nice and safe. No open windows, okay?"

Disappointment settled as she imagined her father's dejected expression when he realized he wouldn't be receiving a visit today. Both she and her dad were imprisoned, forced to serve time for a crime they didn't commit.

Ryan traced a finger very tenderly along her cheek, just below the cut that had been made by the attacker's knife.

"That's healing quickly," he said. "It's looking good."

She turned her head away, feeling awkward under his touch and remembering her resolve not to grow too close to him. Kitty couldn't imagine herself ever becoming close to a man, since she could give her heart only to someone who was truly on her side. And what man would place his trust in the daughter of Harry Linklater, the most hated man in the entire state?

"I'll check in by phone every hour," Ryan said, making his way to the door. "If you don't pick up, I'll come straight over."

"I'll make sure to pick up. I don't want to waste any more of your time."

He stopped in the hallway. "You're not wasting my time, Kitty. So don't ever think that way."

She crossed her arms as if defending herself against the sincere kindness in his voice. She didn't want to be drawn to his caring nature. He clearly wasn't her true ally. She had no allies.

Ryan stepped out into the drizzly day and stood on the deck, hands on his belt. For a moment, he looked just like one of the statues outside the county museum, noble and dignified and upright.

"Stay inside and keep warm," he said. "And—"

She cut him off. "And don't forget to lock up behind you."

He smiled. "I know I sound like a stuck record, but it's because I care."

They stood in silence for a second or two before Ryan walked to his truck. He waved to her, then set off down the lane.

Shadow came running across the yard, crying for attention, so Kitty picked him up, burying her face in the cat's soft fur. Her feelings for Ryan were troubling and complex and most definitely unwanted.

The question was—how could she rid herself of them?

Ryan picked up a dead bolt from the shelf at the hardware store, pleased that it felt weighty and strong in his hand. The door to the new panic room in Kitty's home was pretty tough, but it wouldn't hurt to add an extra layer of protection.

He walked to the counter and set the bolt down, then reached for his wallet.

Buzz nodded a greeting and rang up the price on the till. "Is this for Kitty's house?" he asked, taking Ryan's payment.

"Would you still sell it to me if I said yes?" Ryan replied.

"I would."

"Then yes, it's for Kitty's house."

Buzz handed him his change. "A friend of mine who works in the big hardware store in Lawton says you ordered one of their security doors a couple of days ago. He says it was real expensive."

Ryan rolled his eyes. Rural communities had a grapevine where news spread like a forest fire.

"So what kind of setup does Kitty have down at the lake house?" Buzz asked. "It must be like a fortress, huh?"

"It's secure," Ryan said. "Why do you want to know?"

Buzz shrugged. "Just curious. If someone's out to get her then she can't go taking any chances."

Ryan put the bolt back down on the counter. "What do you know about someone being out to get Kitty, Buzz?"

"Nothing much," he said. "Only I know her front door got shot up and kicked in a few days ago. I delivered a new one from our warehouse if you remember."

"Who told you that her front door was shot up?"

"You did."

"No, I didn't. I told you that someone tried to break in. I didn't tell you he shot through the door." Ryan folded his arms. "So how come you knew?"

Buzz looked a little like a child being reprimanded, guilty, as though he had done something wrong.

"Well, the old door was on the ground, all splintered and cracked, so I just put two and two together," Buzz said. "It looked like a gun attack to me."

This was a plausible explanation, but something about Buzz's cagey demeanor made Ryan's senses prickle to attention. Buzz was avoiding eye contact, bowing his head, revealing tiny flecks of white in his hair—flecks that looked suspiciously like paint.

"Have you been painting, Buzz?" Ryan asked.

"No, sir."

"What's that in your hair?"

Buzz lifted a hand and rubbed his scalp, confusion evident on his face. "I don't know what you mean," he said. "There's nothing in my hair."

"Somebody spray painted a message on Kitty's barn recently. You wouldn't happen to know anything about that, would you?"

"No, sir."

Ryan pulled out his cellphone, deciding that this conversation needed to be recorded. "Can

I ask where you were on Tuesday morning, at approximately 2:00 a.m.?"

A voice echoed from the staircase that led to the Prices' home above the store. "He was at home, sleeping in his bed, Chief Deputy."

Frank's footsteps could be heard on the stairs. When he appeared, his face was angry, jaw clenched and eyes tight.

"Ain't you got anything better to do than harass the good people of this town?" he said, putting his arm around his grandson, sending Ryan a clear message that Buzz was off-limits. "You're so obsessed with protecting Kitty Linklater that you see danger everywhere, even in this decent young man here. We recently had Deputy Harmon knocking on our door with a bunch of questions. Now we've got you bothering us, too."

Ryan's hackles rose at the insinuation that he was behaving unprofessionally.

"I'm not obsessed with Kitty," he said defensively. "Crimes are being committed and it's my duty to investigate them. Shane is going house to house, so you're not being singled out in any way. I just noticed that Buzz has some flecks of white paint in his hair and I want to know why. It's a simple enough question."

"Buzz was helping me paint an old cabinet yesterday," Frank said. "He probably got some splashes in his hair that will take a while to wash out." He smiled unpleasantly. "Painting old cabinets isn't a crime, so you got no business interrogating my grandson."

Frank's mop of white, curly hair gave him the appearance of a kindly old man, but appearances were deceptive, because at only fifty-nine years of age, Frank was anything but old and certainly not kindly.

"I'm not accusing Buzz of being a criminal," Ryan said. "I'm making inquiries."

Frank walked to the front door, opened it wide and said, "Well, go and make your inquiries elsewhere, because you're not welcome in this store anymore."

With a sigh of reluctant acceptance, Ryan picked up his dead bolt, tipped his hat politely and stepped out onto the sidewalk. The door was promptly slammed behind him and the blind pulled down. Frank was like a gatekeeper for his grandson and now would be watching Buzz like a hawk, never allowing Ryan near him.

"Hey, boss," Shane called out, standing in the doorway of the station a little farther down the street. "I'm guessing you diverted your cell to the office—there's a personal call for you."

"I'm on my way," he said, slipping the bolt into his pocket.

When he stepped into the station, Shane

handed him the phone with a knowing smile. "Kitty Linklater for you, sir."

Ryan took the handset with a feeling of annoyance. It was becoming apparent that the town of Bethesda was gossiping about him and Kitty. It was unfair.

"Hello, Kitty," he said. "Everything okay?"

"Yeah, there's no problem here. I just wanted to add you to Dad's visitor list for tomorrow. It usually takes a few days for approval, but with you being a member of law enforcement, the prison officials said they'll be fine with you coming along. I only need to know your badge number."

He took a moment to fully understand what she was saying. Did she really think he intended to accompany her inside the prison, to sit with her father, to look him in the eye?

"I think there's been a misunderstanding," he said. "I never wanted to meet your father. I'll wait outside for you, in the truck."

"Oh," she said with clear disappointment. "Why didn't you say so before? I told you earlier that I'd be calling the prison to let them know we'll be visiting tomorrow. Why would I do that if not to add you to the list? I wouldn't need to tell them that I'm visiting—I'm already on the approved list."

"Perhaps I wasn't paying close enough attention to what you were saying, but there's no way I'd ever agree to be on your father's visitor list."

"Why not?"

"I refuse to sit at the same table as a child killer." He knew his tone was harsh. "Under no circumstances will I meet your father."

He heard a sharp intake of breath on the other end of the line. "I know how you feel about my dad, but I thought you could take this opportunity to see for yourself what kind of man he is. He's—"

"No," Ryan said, stopping her before she could finish her sentence. "I know what kind of a man he is. I don't need to look into his eyes to confirm it."

"Please, Ryan. If you could just give him one minute of your time, I'd be really grateful. If you never want to see him again after that, I'll respect your decision."

Ryan rubbed his forehead, his agitation increasing. "Maybe I'm not making myself clear here, Kitty. Your dad is in the same prison as the man who killed my sister. And they're both where they belong. Neither of them deserves any visitors at all, in my view." An image of Gina flashed across his mind, her pigtails trailing in the wind as she ran. "If you want to visit a man who murdered a beautiful young girl, then that's your right, but I choose to stay away."

She went quiet for a while. "Look, I caught you off guard with this—you're making a snap decision. We can talk later. Will you at least think about it?"

"No, I won't think about it, and neither will I change my mind. It's not just about my personal feelings. I also have my professional reputation to think about. If the prison officials see me visiting Harry Linklater, they'll assume I'm crazy or stupid. Or both."

"When you made the decision to rent the apartment, you said your reputation could take a hit." Annoyance was creeping into her voice. "Or was that a lie?"

"The warden of Oklahoma Penitentiary knows me well, and he's been good to me and my family over the years, keeping us informed of any developments in Cody Jones's parole hearings. I would be ashamed if he saw me visiting a child killer."

"Do you think I should be ashamed of myself?" she asked, her voice eerily flat and calm, perhaps holding back a flood of anger.

"That's a matter for your own conscience," he said.

"I see," she hissed. "If that's how you feel, then perhaps it would be a good idea if you found someplace else to live. I'll raise the money for the new cellar door and pay you back."

Ryan realized that he had perhaps gone too far and had failed to understand the situation from her side of the fence. Kitty wasn't being intentionally difficult—she was simply speaking her version of the truth.

"Don't be rash. I think you're a good person who tries very hard to do the right thing. It's your father I have an issue with, not you."

"It amounts to the same thing in my mind," she said, her voice rising. "If you have an issue with my dad, you have an issue with me. I can't believe I was stupid enough to think this arrangement would work out."

"Okay, let's take a breather and talk about this later. We both need to calm down."

"I'm perfectly calm," she yelled ironically. "I don't want to talk about this later. In fact, I don't want to talk to you for the rest of the day, so please don't call because I won't pick up."

Ryan had let this conversation get way out of control.

"You're putting your life in danger because we had a fight?" he said. "That's crazy."

"Haven't you worked it out by now, Ryan?" she shouted. "I *am* crazy. Just ask anyone in Bethesda and they'll tell you I'm the crackpot daughter of a local murderer."

"Please don't do this, Kitty."

But she had already clicked off the phone.

"Trouble in paradise, huh, boss?" Shane said with a smirk.

Ryan shot him a look that told the deputy to back off. "Don't start, Shane."

Placing the phone back on the receiver, Ryan wondered whether Kitty would go through with her threat to evict him. He wasn't sure. But the worst part was that the thought of being freed from her complicated, problematic life actually made him relieved. He never wanted to argue with her about her repugnant father again, or justify his living arrangements to the sheriff, or suffer the knowing smirks of Shane. Leaving the Linklater house behind would not only lift a burden, but would ensure he could successfully be elected county sheriff.

But then his mind conjured up a vision of Kitty's face, with the tiny cut running across one cheek, and her dark eyes imploring someone to help her. However much he wanted to be rid of the difficulties she'd created in his life, he could never abandon her. Not until she was safe.

Kitty screamed into the silence, a long guttural wail that let out all her frustration and fury. How could she ever have worried about allowing herself to get too close to Ryan? It should've been obvious that sooner or later they would have a big bust-up.

She paced the hallway like a caged animal, arms crossed and lips pinched, breathing hard. How dare Ryan imply that she should be ashamed of visiting her father. He was letting his background cloud his judgment again, and she was deeply hurt by his comments. She wanted to understand his point of view, but she also desperately wanted him to give her father a chance. There was no way she and Ryan could live under the same roof with such fundamental differences. She resolved to enforce a move-out day. She'd find a way to manage financially without him.

"I gotta get out of here," she said out loud, feeling the walls close in on her.

She snatched up her car keys and contemplated leaving the house. Home felt restrictive…but also safe. Her pulse began racing at the thought of venturing outside alone.

"You can do this, Kitty," she told herself. "Nothing bad has happened in almost two days."

But a little voice rang inside her head, saying, *Two days isn't a long time.*

She hung the keys back on the hook and turned to walk into the kitchen, feeling her heart sink at her lack of courage and her lack of conviction in her own ability to protect herself. How on earth was she going to manage without Ryan in the house if she didn't even have the confidence to step outside the front door?

"This is ridiculous," she said, picking up her purse from a chair in the kitchen. "I have to learn to take care of myself."

She unzipped the purse, took out her gun, checked that it was loaded and carefully placed it back inside. She also checked that her cell was fully charged and that she had enough money for gas. Then she slung the bag over her shoulder, picked up her coat and walked down the hallway.

Slowly and with trepidation, she opened the front door, feeling the cool, moist wind blow into her face. She realized she was trembling as she stepped out onto the porch.

"I'm strong and capable," she said, bolstering herself. "I don't need a bodyguard."

She took the gun out of her purse and placed it in her pocket. She intended to keep it the glove box of the car while she drove. And she intended to drive all the way to Oklahoma State Penitentiary, a journey of almost three hours that should see her arrive just as afternoon visiting hours began. With her wits about her and her gun within reach, she could be there and back by dinnertime.

Behind the closed front door, she heard the phone ringing and waited until the machine picked up. Then, as she had anticipated, her cell began to buzz in her purse. She fished it out and looked at the display. It was the number of the sheriff's office.

Hitting the answer button, she said, "I asked you not to call me today."

"You didn't pick up the home telephone."

"I already told you I wouldn't."

"Did you leave the house?"

"No." That wasn't a lie, not while her feet were still on the porch.

"Please don't do anything rash, Kitty. I'm worried about you."

"Listen, Ryan," she said. "I appreciate your concern, but I'm busy, so unless you have something important to say, I'd like to get on with my day."

"Sure," he said. "You'll call if there's any trouble?"

"Of course."

She clicked off the phone without an ounce of regret for neglecting to tell him her plans. His earlier cruel words about her father still lingered in her ears. Ryan might be ashamed to visit her father, but she certainly wasn't. She would march into that prison with her head held high.

She didn't need Ryan's approval. She didn't need anybody's approval.

* * *

Ryan stood in the window of the station watching Price's Hardware Store, hoping to spot anything that might be considered suspicious. He wasn't sure exactly what he was looking for, but his gut told him that Buzz was hiding something.

"What can you tell me about the Price family?" Ryan asked Shane.

"They're proud people," he replied. "After the scandal of both of Buzz's parents running off and abandoning him, they kind of keep to themselves."

"And what do you think of Buzz? Is he a good kid in your opinion?"

"For sure, but he's bullied by his grandpa." Shane brushed crumbs from his shirt. "Frank's got a mean temper on him, and Sheila and Buzz bear the brunt."

Ryan turned around. "Do you think Frank ever gets physical with them?"

"I believe so. Sheila sometimes has bruises, but she clams up whenever I press the matter. It's hard to get close to her, and believe me, I've tried."

Ryan had seen Sheila Price just once, a small, birdlike woman who scurried away from his presence when he went to introduce himself in the store. He vowed to check up on her and ensure she was okay.

He watched Carla Torlioni sweep the sidewalk outside her café and inspect the potted plants, her white apron stretching taut over her plump figure as she leaned over. When she noticed him looking at her, she stuck her chin in the air. Frank came out of his store and went to join her, pointing at Ryan and talking energetically. Carla shook her head and pursed her lips, all for Ryan's benefit, he was sure.

"I don't think I'm very popular with people in this town, Shane," he said.

Shane pushed his chair away from the desk and wheeled it over to the window to peer out.

"Oh, don't worry about those two," he said. "They don't like anybody. A town like this isn't easy to crack, but you'll get there. There are plenty of good folks here. Paul and Nancy from the grocery store tell everybody how impressed they are with your professionalism."

Ryan raised his eyebrows in surprise. "They do?"

"Yeah, and it's getting to be a little annoying, if I'm being honest. I've been working in this town for ten years and the nicest thing anybody said about me is that I smell good."

Ryan sniffed the air and laughed. "And even they were lying."

Shane put a hand on his chest, mimicking being wounded. "That was harsh, boss...but you're probably right."

The phone rang and Shane rose from his chair. "I've got it."

Ryan focused his attention on the street again. Frank and Carla had been joined by her husband, and Joe was encouraging her to go back inside, while she resisted. Joe had given Ryan a statement regarding the recent incident in the woods, but he wasn't surprised that Carla had not.

"I'm sorry," Shane was saying into the receiver. "I can't make out a word. Do you want to talk to Chief Deputy Lawrence?"

Shane held the receiver toward Ryan. "It's a bad line, but I think he asked for you."

Ryan took the phone. "This is Ryan Lawrence. How can I help you?"

The voice that replied was deep, gravelly and distorted, leading Ryan to immediately suspect that it might be channeled through a voice changer.

"Kitty Linklater is in danger."

"Who is this?"

"That's not important. Kitty will be run off the road today unless you help her."

"But she's at home."

"No, she's not. She's on the highway, probably headed to the prison, and she'll be attacked on her way back."

Ryan was dumbstruck for a second. Would Kitty lie to him, drive almost three hours on her own and put herself at serious risk? He needed no time to consider the answer. Of course she would.

"Where will she be run off the road?" he asked, snatching up his keys. "Tell me exactly where?"

"I don't know. It could be anywhere, so quit talking and get moving."

"I need more information. What highway?"

But the man had hung up. And Ryan's chest burst with fear and dread. Kitty was driving right into a trap.

"What route does Kitty take to and from the prison?" he asked Shane. "Do you know?"

The deputy wrinkled his brow, thinking. "She once mentioned that she likes a rest stop on Highway 1. It's just outside the town of Allen, called something like Toasty Cabin. Head out toward that." He checked his watch. "Prison visiting hours are just about to end, so if she's there, she'll be leaving in five minutes or so."

"Stay here and hold the fort," Ryan said, opening the door. "If that guy calls back, contact me on the emergency radio channel immediately."

"What else can I do to help?" Shane asked,

recognizing the severity of the situation. "I can't just sit here, doing nothing."

"You can say a prayer," Ryan called as he ran to his truck. "Kitty's gonna need it."

SIX

Kitty breathed in the crisp, fresh air outside the Oklahoma State Penitentiary, trying to stem her flow of tears. She had no idea when her father would be able to experience the perfect joy of breathing free air again, and she was worried that he was beginning to lose hope. He was becoming very thin and frail, clearly not eating enough. He'd smiled and pretended he was doing fine, but she saw right through it. His despondency had increased her motivation to work harder.

She started up the car, switched on her phone and placed it on the passenger seat before setting off. It bleeped several times, letting her know that someone was trying to reach her, most likely Ryan checking on her. She decided to return his calls after figuring out how she would broach the subject of the apartment. She didn't want to provoke another fight, but she had to be firm about her feelings. It required careful consideration. Glancing at the display on the cell, she saw that she had missed several calls, and smiled a little smugly. Ryan had no need to worry about her. After all, she was successfully proving to him that she could manage her own safety.

She turned up the radio, wound her way through the streets of McAlester and then headed onto the rural highway that would take her home. The journey took her through some beautiful little towns dotted along the way, but she had to struggle to enjoy the scenic views, knowing that her father was behind bars, counting the minutes until her next visit.

The sign for her favorite rest stop, the Cozy Cabin, was very welcome when it came into view. Kitty was definitely ready to refuel both her body and the car. She turned onto the road that led to the rustic establishment, noticing a black car approaching rapidly from the rear. She tried to tuck herself onto the shoulder, giving the vehicle plenty of room to pass, but the driver continued coming toward her with what appeared to be malicious intent.

"Go around," she said, putting her arm out the window and trying to wave him past.

But he didn't go around her and didn't slow down. Kitty braced for the inevitable impact, hunching her shoulders and gripping the wheel as if her life depended on it.

The crunch of metal on metal was horrible and her car jerked forward on the asphalt, veering from side to side. She struggled to maintain control, slamming the gas pedal to the floor in an attempt to flee. The small engine of her car whined, managing a pathetic top speed that would never rival the more powerful vehicle on her tail.

"Oh, Lord," she said aloud. "I need You now."

Then she was slammed again and the force of the impact was enough to deploy her airbag. Kitty screamed as the huge white balloon rose up in her face, causing her to lose sight of the road. Her car skidded out of control until she didn't know which way was forward. She seemed to be spinning like a top, totally at the mercy of the momentum.

She came to rest in a ditch filled with muddy water, cold and shocking against her warm skin. She panicked, fearing that she would drown, and fumbled to undo the buckle of her seat belt. But she couldn't find the button beneath the water and began to shout for help. Thankfully, it took only a minute for rational thought to reassert itself and show her that the water level was only to her waist.

The danger in this situation wasn't drowning—the true danger hadn't yet revealed itself.

Finally getting herself free from the seat belt,

Kitty tried to crane her neck to check the location of the black car. She couldn't see it, but heard footsteps on the asphalt. She reached beneath the waterline to open the glove compartment, but she fumbled in her panic and the weapon slithered through her fingers. Her cell was somewhere under the water, too, having fallen from the passenger seat into the murk.

Then the sweetest sound reached her ears: a siren. It was heading her way. She would need to flag down the emergency vehicle before it passed; that was perhaps her only chance of survival.

After scrambling through the open window of the car, she splashed through the ditch water and climbed up the bank to the road, where she saw her attacker walking toward her. She stared at him, horrified, his masked face hiding all but his small eyes. It took her a second or two to register that he was pointing a gun at her and she found herself frozen to the spot, her muddy, wet pants dripping onto the dry ground.

Her attacker said, almost imperceptibly, "I'm sorry for this," and calmly squeezed the trigger. She screamed, wondering if she would feel any pain or if it would be quick. Nothing happened. Instead of a gunshot resounding through the air, the man's swearing filled the space. His gun had jammed. As the siren grew louder and louder, she watched him furiously hurl the weapon through the window of his car before climbing in and squealing off in the opposite direction. Then she allowed herself to fall back onto the road, flat on her back, arms out to the side, recovering her breath.

That was her closest escape yet.

Ryan's truck screeched to a halt next to Kitty's car, which was listing on its side in a ditch. He'd spotted the car while racing along Highway 1, and his stomach had lurched at the sight of the damage. Kitty herself was lying on the road, breathing hard, her chest rising and falling hard.

He jumped from the truck. "Are you okay, Kitty? Please say you're okay."

"I'm okay."

He dropped to his knees at her side, noticing that she was shivering in her wet clothes.

"We'll get you to a hospital," he said. "You should be checked over."

"I don't need a hospital. I'm fine," she said, sitting up. "But I'd be dead by now if that guy's gun hadn't jammed."

"I saw a black car speed past me on the highway just now. Is the driver the man who did this?"

"Yeah," she said, sitting up with a groan.

"He came out of nowhere and rammed me from behind."

"I put out a radio alert already, so let's hope he gets picked up soon. Who was it? Did you know him or recognize the car?"

She shook her head. "He was wearing a mask again, and it all happened so fast, I didn't have time to get a good look at anything. But the weirdest thing is that he apologized to me before trying to fire the gun."

Ryan helped her to her feet, keeping his senses alert in case the suspect came back for a second attempt.

"How did you know I was in trouble?" she asked. "Your arrival can't have been a coincidence."

"I got a tip-off. Somebody called the station and said you'd be run off the road on your way back from the prison. It's fortunate that I got to the right place at the right time."

"You got a tip-off? Who was it?"

"I'm pretty sure it was a man's voice, but it was being channeled through a distorter, so he wants to remain anonymous."

Kitty walked to Ryan's truck and leaned against it, her color gradually returning. "What did he say?"

"He said you'd made a trip to the prison today and would be attacked on the way home." Now that Ryan had established Kitty's well-being, he was finding it hard to contain his annoyance. "At first I thought it must be a prank, because I figured there was no way you'd come all this way without telling anyone where you're going. I mean, nobody is that reckless, right?"

Kitty looked at the ground. "I thought I could handle it," she said quietly. "I wanted to prove that I could take care of myself, that I didn't need you."

How could he say this diplomatically? "But you *do* need me."

She appeared unusually reticent as she replied, "I have to learn to get by without you."

"Okay," he said, uncertain exactly what she meant. "But you have to rely on someone, because you can't do this on your own. You need someone watching out for you."

She nodded, apparently accepting his words.

"I must've called your cell twenty times or more," he said. "Why didn't you answer?"

"My phone was off while I was in the prison. When I turned it back on as I was leaving, I saw the missed calls but I didn't realize you were trying to warn me."

"I was hoping to steer you away from danger, to get you to stay at the prison until I arrived. The man who's targeting you is always waiting for the right time to strike. And you gave him that opening by coming here alone. You can't put your life on the line like this just to make a point."

"I wasn't making a point," she said. "I was visiting my dad."

"I think you were doing both."

She said nothing, crossing her arms and pressing her lips shut.

"I understand how hard it must be relying on my protection," he said. "Especially when we fight and you resent me."

"I don't resent you," she said.

He raised an eyebrow. "You don't?"

"Well, okay, maybe a little, but you really hurt my feelings today and as a result, I made a hasty decision. I know this is my fault and I've been careless. You don't need to rub it in."

"I don't mean to make you feel bad," he said, putting a hand on her shoulder. "I just want you to understand that you can't always assume you'll be okay. Am I right that you didn't tell anybody else where you were going today?"

She nodded.

"Did anybody see you leave town?" he asked. "Did you stop anywhere along the way?"

"I stopped at the gas station just outside town. Frank Price was there filling up his delivery truck. He asked me if I was headed off to the prison."

"What did you tell him?"

"To mind his own business."

"Frank could've told any number of people that he saw you in your car, heading in this direction." He imagined the grapevine of Bethesda set in motion. "And somehow your attacker got word of your whereabouts and guessed your destination. But fortunately for us, he told someone else of his plans and that Good Samaritan decided to do the right thing and warn us. If it weren't for his intervention…"

He didn't finish the sentence. He didn't need to.

"That mystery caller saved my life today. And you, of course."

He smiled. "It's getting to be a habit, huh?"

She closed her eyes and let her head fall against the door of the truck behind her as a fine rain began to fall.

"You're right," she admitted. "I do hate having to rely on you for protection. I hate that I'm forced to place my faith in a man who doesn't believe in my father's goodness. I wanted to prove that I didn't need you." She opened her eyes and looked over at her car in the ditch. "But I clearly do need you, no matter how much I wish it wasn't true."

"Don't beat yourself up about it," he said, standing directly in front of her and resting his hands on her shoulders. "You're not a trained member of law enforcement. You've never been shown how to deal with assailants or how to repel an attack. It's not shameful to need help. And I want to help you—keep you safe." He took a deep breath. "The fact that I don't believe in your father's innocence is something we'll have to learn to live with. I'm really sorry we're not on the same page, but that's just the way it is."

He watched her crinkle her brow. He sensed there was a lot she wanted to say but didn't dare. And he felt much the same way. They were standing close together but were so very far apart.

"I'd decided earlier on that I was going to ask you to move out of the apartment," she said. "I didn't want to continue sharing my house with someone who thinks I'm wasting my time fighting my father's case."

"And do you still feel the same way?"

"No."

"Good. Because I've got nowhere else to go, and Frank Price has probably bad-mouthed me all over town by now so I might not get another local rental."

"Why would Frank do that?"

Ryan told her about the conversation he'd had in Price's Hardware, about the paint in Buzz's hair and Frank's insistence that Ryan leave the store and never return.

Her eyes widened. "Do you think Buzz painted the message on the barn?"

"I don't know, but he's definitely holding something back. I'll be watching him carefully from now on. We're getting closer to the truth every day, Kitty, so just give me a little longer to track this guy down. Once we've got him caught, I'll move out."

The rain had begun to settle on her olive skin, giving it a dewy sheen, and a tiny droplet hung from her chin.

"It's not that I don't want you in the apartment, Ryan," she said, wiping the moisture from her cheeks. "It's just that it's tough listening to you tearing down my belief in my father. It's hard enough fighting against the town every day. I don't need that negativity at home, as well."

It was becoming clear that his comments were taking a heavy toll on Kitty, much heavier than he'd appreciated. And he felt bad for it.

"Okay, I hear you," he said, taking off his jacket and putting it around her shoulders. "I'll try my best to keep my opinions to myself."

"I know why that's difficult for you, what with your past," she said. "You don't often mention your sister, but I'm sure she's never far from your mind."

He found his jaw clenching. "I don't like to talk about Gina. It makes me think of how she died, and who killed her."

He turned his head in the direction of the penitentiary, where Cody Jones had been languishing for many years, and hopefully, where he would languish for many more to come.

"My dad always used to say that holding a grudge is like drinking poison and expecting the other person to die," Kitty said. "It makes no sense."

Ryan walked away from her. "I'm not holding a grudge."

"Okay," she said. "But if you ever want to talk about it, I'm a good listener."

He stopped himself from laughing to avoid hurting her feelings. Did she realize how ridiculous it was to suggest that he confide his innermost thoughts about Gina to the daughter of a child murderer?

"Thanks, Kitty," he said. "But I'm doing fine. Now let's get you home and dry, and I'll check if any patrols have located the black car."

"My purse, gun and cell phone are in my car," she said. "They're under the water."

"I'll get them for you. It's not good for guns to be immersed but if I retrieve it quick, it should be fine once it's dried out. I'm not sure about the cell."

"What about the car?"

He performed a cursory inspection of the bodywork. "I'll organize a tow truck, but my guess is that it's wrecked beyond repair."

She pulled the jacket tighter around her shoulders. "It's not the only thing a wreck. That was way too close a call."

He opened the driver's door and plunged his hand into the cold, dirty water, feeling for the items she needed. She was right about this latest incident being too close a call. He hoped she now fully understood that danger of this magnitude couldn't be treated flippantly. It demanded respect.

His determination to save her would have to match her attacker's determination to kill her.

Kitty placed a log on the fire and watched the sparks dance into the chimney. She had taken a long, hot shower and changed into fleecy sweatpants and an oversize hoodie, but she couldn't seem to get warm. And neither could she wash the day away. Its menace lingered all around her, the barrel of her attacker's gun now imprinted on her mind.

"You feeling a little better now?" Ryan asked, coming into the room with a large mug of hot chocolate and setting it on the coffee table. "Your color's returned so that's a good sign."

"Every time I close my eyes, I see him," she said. "Standing there in the road, pulling the trigger, with his gun aimed right at my head."

Ryan sat on the chair closest to the fire, where Kitty was kneeling next to the warmth. "Try not to think about it too much."

"I'm guessing that you weren't able to trace the car?"

His expression of disappointment said it all. "The plate turned out to be false, but we're sure about the make and model, and there are only so many of them in the county. I put out another alert to all officers in the area. They're running through the list of registered owners, and keeping an eye on the roads. Let's hope one of them picks him up tonight."

Ryan had changed out of his uniform since returning home and now wore jeans and a chunky, patterned sweater, the kind knitted by grandmas for Christmas. The green color suited his red hair and matched his eyes, making him appear somehow softer and cuter. Right at that moment he didn't look like a law enforcement officer. He looked like a kindergarten teacher.

She picked up the hot chocolate, which Ryan had topped with marshmallows, one of her favorite treats.

"So who do you think our mystery informant is?" she asked, lifting a gooey marshmallow from the mug. "Did he give you any clues?"

"It was impossible to judge what his real voice sounds like, so it could be anyone, but the accent was definitely local."

"It would have to be someone that my attacker confided in," she said. "It may even be a friend of his. So if we can identify the informant, we'll get closer to identifying the attacker."

"I'm not getting my hopes up," Ryan said. "The caller blocked his number, and with no other information available, I've got no leads at all."

"But it's a good sign," she said, feeling a shiver of excitement at the significance of this latest development. "If our informant is a friend of my attacker, then he probably also knows that this guy is Molly's real killer."

Ryan remained silent.

"Don't you see what this means?" she said, letting her eagerness get the better of her. "The man who tipped you off today could be the key to solving Molly's murder. He's the breakthrough I've been waiting for. We have to find him."

Ryan's stared at his hands, clearly unwilling to speak.

"Oh yeah," she said. "I forgot. You think the real killer is in prison already."

"I think you're reaching too far," he said. "The informant could be anybody. We don't know that your attacker confided in him about this or anything else. He could've happened to have overheard a conversation and decided to make the call. I'm not shooting your entire theory down in flames, but let's not assume anything."

"The only part you're shooting down in flames is the part where my dad turns out to be wrongfully convicted, right?"

"All I'm saying is that we shouldn't jump to conclusions."

Ryan didn't want her using this mystery man to bolster her crazy belief in her father's innocence. But true to his word, he was trying hard not to trample on her feelings and had diplomatically avoided asserting her father's guilt.

She put her mug down on the table. "Okay, so tell me again exactly what the guy said. Can you remember?"

"He really didn't say much at all," replied Ryan. "He said you were in danger, that you'd be run off the road on your way back from the prison. When I asked some questions he told me to quit talking and get moving."

"He said those exact words? 'Quit talking and get moving'? Are you sure?"

"Yeah I'm sure. Why? Do you think you might know him?"

She shook her head, quelling the fizz in her belly, uncertain whether she wanted to confide in Ryan. She knew someone who used that expression frequently, but she doubted that Ryan would support her theory. And he would be unlikely to investigate as thoroughly as she would. Kitty was a trained investigative journalist, after all. She might not know how to fight an assailant but she knew how to dig for the truth.

"I'll make a call to Nancy from the grocery store tomorrow," she said, trying to sound offhand. "She might know someone who uses that expression."

"Don't tell her why you want to know," Ryan said gravely. "We should keep this under wraps for now."

"Sure." She hated deceiving him, but his lack of faith in her judgment propelled her to follow up on this alone. "I'll keep it all under wraps."

Kitty was quiet after dinner, unusually so. Ryan had cooked her a meal while she rested and then asked if he could remain with her for the evening, to check she suffered no ill effects from the car crash. She seemed lost in thought, curled up on the sofa, staring into the fire.

"Is everything okay?" he asked. "Are you sure you're okay with me being here? I can go to my apartment if you prefer."

"You're fine to stay," she said. "Thanks for making dinner. I didn't have the energy to cook."

"It's been a tough day, huh?"

"Yes, it has. It's given me a lot to think about."

Her voice was flat and expressionless, her usual enthusiasm and motivation having apparently vanished.

"Are you sure you're okay?"

She took her gaze away from the fire and settled it on him. "If I uncover some new evidence that supports my father's claim of innocence, will you help me investigate it?"

"Well, that would all depend on what it was." He narrowed his eyes. "Why do you ask? Do you have something in mind?"

She looked away, back into the fire. "No, but you never know what might crop up."

"Are you talking about the informant?" He suspected that she had gotten her hopes up, after all. "Because we have no way of tracking him down, not unless he calls again."

"Okay," she said, running her fingers through her loose hair. "Let's talk hypothetically. If we track down the informant and he claims to know who really killed Molly, would you be willing to change your mind about my father?"

"I can't comment on something that hasn't happened," he said. "The informant didn't say anything about Molly's killer."

She let out a growl of frustration, covering her face with her hands, her voice muffled behind her palms as she said, "I was talking hypothetically. You drive me crazy, you know that?"

He sighed. "I'm sorry I can't give you what you want, Kitty. I can't be the ally you need because my sympathies don't lie with Cody Jones. My sympathies lie with the Thomas family and everyone who's been hurt by Molly's murder."

She tilted her head and looked at him quizzically. "What did you just say?"

"I said that my sympathies don't lie with your father."

"No, you didn't. You said that your sympathies don't lie with Cody Jones."

Did he? It must've been a slip of the tongue. "You know what I meant."

She eyeballed him. "Cody Jones and my father are *not* the same person, Ryan."

"I know that."

"No, I don't think you do. When you think of my father, whose face do you see?"

Ryan tried to recall the mug shot of Harry Linklater, an image he'd seen in the newspaper numerous times, but was unable to remember his features. Instead, the face of Cody Jones settled on his mind, the killer's mouth curled in a satisfied sneer.

"I don't see anyone's face," he said, thinking

that a little white lie would prevent an argument. "I see no one."

She smiled and he instantly understood that she had seen right through him. Despite knowing him such a short amount of time she had learned those little giveaways and tells that he was clearly unaware of.

"Okay," he admitted. "I might sometimes get the two men mixed up, but that doesn't mean I'm wrong about either of them."

"But it means you can't be objective. You can't look at the situation as an impartial observer, and I'll never be able to totally trust you."

He was hurt by this. "You can trust me completely, Kitty."

She shook her head, unfolding her legs from beneath her and sitting up. "I trust you with my safety, but not with everything else. Some things I have to keep to myself."

What did she mean by this? "Is there information that you're keeping from me? Because I promise that I'll help you any way I can."

She stood. "I'm going to bed now."

"But it's only eight thirty."

"I need an early night." She picked up Shadow from the sofa and tucked him under her arm. "Can you switch off the lights when you turn in?"

"Sure."

She walked to the open door, but he felt compelled to call her back. "Kitty."

She turned.

"I really care about you," he said. "I just wanted you to know that."

She nodded and then exited, leaving him with just the glow of the fire for company. He knelt by the hearth and used the poker to reposition a fallen log, thinking about the conversation that had just occurred. He knew the difference between Cody Jones and Harry Linklater. He sometimes struggled to remember which was which, but that wasn't such a terrible mistake, was it? Both were guilty of a similar crime, both immoral men locked up where they belonged.

He refused to feel bad about his mistake in confusing the two. He had done nothing wrong.

Kitty placed Shadow on her bed and pulled her cell from her pocket. After drying the phone by the fire, the only lasting damage appeared to be a thin crack on the screen. Scrolling through her contacts list, she finally located the correct number and hit the call button.

She found herself feeling glad that she had chosen not to confide in Ryan. He would only pour water on her flames. Each time she took a step in the right direction, he came up with a supposedly rational explanation to undercut her discoveries. This time she would not let him ruin a new lead. This time she was onto something big, and she would investigate alone.

Someone finally picked up the receiver. "Hello."

"Hi," she said quietly, being careful not to alert Ryan. "It's Kitty."

There was silence for a few seconds. "What do you want?"

"You called Ryan at the Bethesda station today," she said. "You told him to 'quit talking and get moving'—that's what you always say at the end of the night, isn't it? It's how you get people out of the bar. Stop messing with me. I know it was you. And that means you can identify who's after me. It's time to do the right thing and tell me what you know."

More silence.

"Harvey?" she said. "Are you still there?"

He let out a big sigh, long and sorrowful.

"Can you come over?" he said. "There's something I want you to have."

SEVEN

Kitty gripped the phone receiver tightly, wondering what Harvey could be referring to. Was it worth her while trusting him after everything he'd done? "What do you have for me?" Kitty asked. "Because you owe me, Harvey."

"It's the CCTV footage from the night of Molly's murder. It shows your father arriving at eight in the evening and leaving at two in the morning."

"You told the police that it had been erased," she said, clenching her fist. "You lied."

"Yes, I lied. I'm not expecting forgiveness for what I've done to you and your father, Kitty, but I can at least try to put things right."

"Who killed Molly? You know, don't you?"

"I can't tell you that."

"Why?"

"It's complicated."

"It's complicated?" she said incredulously.

"You just said that you were trying to put things right."

"Look," he said. "I did something real bad a few years ago, bad enough to put me in jail for a long time. But I got away with it."

She began to see what had motivated Harvey's lies to the police.

"Does the killer know what you did?"

"Of course he knows. He was my friend at the time. We did the bad thing together and it's bound us. If I rat him out, he rats *me* out. That's the way it goes. And I don't want to go to prison, Kitty."

Kitty racked her brain to think of the people Harvey had counted as friends over the years. Before he'd allowed his bar to become run-down and seedy, it had been frequented by many of the townsfolk, who used to enjoy quiz nights and live music there. Harvey's old accomplice could be anyone.

"What bad thing did you do?" she asked.

"Don't ask me that, because I won't tell you. I was young and stupid and I needed the money that my friend paid me to help him out. I wish I'd never done it, but I did and I've regretted it ever since."

"What about me, Harvey?" she said. "Your friend is trying to kill me."

"I know, and I'm sorry about that. He told

me about the plan to run you off the road today and get the job done right. I've been trying to persuade him to leave you alone, Kitty, I really have, but he's scared that your investigation will lead you straight to him. He's made up his mind that you have to be eliminated, and nothing will convince him otherwise. That's why I tipped off Ryan today. I don't want to see you hurt."

"But he *will* hurt me if Ryan can't find and arrest him. He's already killed Molly. How can you protect this monster?"

"Don't get me wrong—I hate what he's done. When he turned up at my back door needing to change his bloody clothes after killing Molly, I was totally disgusted. I told him that I wouldn't help him, but he threatened to expose our crime. He told me I'd be thrown in a cell for the rest of my life and he didn't care if the same thing happened to him. So I did something that I'm not proud of."

"You pinned the blame for Molly's murder on my father."

"When the police found out about that text to Molly's friend and started asking questions about Harry, I realized that with his criminal past, he'd be the perfect fall guy, so I didn't corroborate his alibi. And I knew I was the only reliable witness for him that night. I set him up, and I'm truly sorry for that, too."

"But not sorry enough to turn in the real killer?"

"Don't you think I want to help?" he said with obvious frustration. "But I've got my own life to think of, too."

"Please, Harvey," she begged. "Tell me who this person is."

His voice was high and strained. "I can't. I really can't. He's dangerous. I'm leaving town to start over, away from it all."

"So you're just running away?"

"I closed the bar today and I leave tonight. My plan is to disappear and never come back. For your own safety, you should do the same thing."

"How can I disappear? My father is in prison serving time for a crime he didn't commit, and I have to fight for him. I'm staying right here."

"The CCTV footage will almost certainly get Harry an appeal. That's as much as I can do for him. I only hope it's enough."

She heard knocking in the background, and Harvey broke off the conversation to call out, "We're closed!" before returning his attention back to her.

"Listen to me, Kitty, because I'll say this only once. I'll leave a memory stick on the bar, right at the end by the cash register. The front door will be open and you're just gonna come right on in and take that stick. I don't want to talk to you or discuss this any further, got it?"

"When this CCTV footage goes public, the police will want to know why you lied."

"Of course, but they'll hafta find me first. I'll be long gone by the time they come looking."

Kitty's mind raced with the suddenness of this opportunity to prove her father's alibi. She was elated but terrified, galvanized but cautious.

"Can I bring someone to the bar with me?" she asked. "You know it's not safe for me to go out alone."

"I don't want anybody else here, especially the police," he said. "So you can forget about bringing Ryan along for the ride."

"And what if I bring him with me, anyway?"

"I'll be watching you arrive, and if I see you with anybody else, I'll take the stick away and you'll never get the footage. I'll watch and wait for you to leave before I head out of town, just to make sure you're okay."

Kitty felt slightly heartened at Harvey's concern for her well-being, despite her bitterness regarding his lies. But could he ensure she would be safe? She knew she couldn't risk confiding in Ryan if she might lose the chance to free her father. No matter how afraid she was, she had to go, and she had to go alone.

"I'll need to wait until Ryan goes to bed," she said. "So I might not get there until eleven."

"That's fine by me. The door will be open."

"This isn't a trap, is it, Harvey? You wouldn't do that to me, would you?"

"It's not a trap," he replied. "I know my promises don't count for much, but you have my word on that."

"Okay. I'll be there soon. And I'll be alone."

Kitty drove slowly and carefully along Main Street toward the Starlight Bar. As her car was out of action, she had been forced to push her father's old pickup out of the garage. After a year of it sitting idle, the battery was weak, but the truck was her only option.

She was experiencing a mixture of dread and excitement, knowing that she could be minutes away from receiving proof to clear her dad. Perhaps she could even persuade Harvey to give up the name of the man he was protecting. But even as a smile curled her lips, fear forced her features into a frown. She didn't have the memory stick in her hand yet.

The Starlight Bar came into view, its distinctive exterior rising up at the very end of Main Street. The black building was covered with tiny white spiked shapes, meant to resemble stars in the night sky, but the decorations were weather-beaten and faded, long since past their best. Harvey spent practically nothing on maintaining his bar, and it had been losing customers for years.

Turning into the parking lot, the first thing Kitty noticed was the smell of smoke. Then she saw a plume of it snaking from the open door, curling upward into the dark sky.

"Oh no," she said, jumping from the truck and pulling her cell from her pocket. "No, no, no!"

She dialed 9-1-1, requesting the fire department and an ambulance. She didn't know whether Harvey was inside or if he needed medical attention. Surely he hadn't started the fire himself? Something sinister must have happened.

"Come on, Kitty," she said, taking her gun from her purse. "Be brave."

She held the weapon close to her chest, finger on the trigger, and approached the door.

"Harvey!" she yelled into the entryway. "Are you here?"

No reply. There was nothing else for it—she had to go inside. Not only might Harvey need help, but the memory stick was on the bar and she couldn't let it be damaged or destroyed.

She ran back to the pickup, pulled a cloth from the glove box and wetted it with some water from an outside tap, before holding it over her mouth. Then she walked slowly though the doorway, feeling her way along the wall in the dark. As soon as she entered the wide open space where tables and chairs sat, she saw a bright orange glow lighting up the bar area, and a searing heat hit her full in the face. The entire wooden bar was ablaze, sending the mirrored stars that covered the ceiling crashing to the floor. Bottles were cracking and smashing under the intense heat, and Kitty had to struggle to breathe behind her makeshift mask. There was no way she could retrieve a memory stick from this inferno—assuming it hadn't been taken or destroyed already. It would be lost forever.

But something worse was to come, because then she saw Harvey. He was lying flat on his back in the middle of the room, a gun resting in one hand and a cell phone in the other. She dropped to her knees and crawled to his side, coughing as smoke fought its way into her lungs.

"Harvey," she mumbled through her cloth, placing her gun on the floor and touching his face. "Say something."

But Harvey could say nothing, thanks to the deep hole in the side of his skull, undeniably made with a bullet. His blood was soaking through the floor, sticky and wet on the knees of her pants. He had been murdered.

A surge of panic and adrenaline coursed through her veins and she scrambled to her feet, snatching up her gun, stumbling and falling in her haste to escape. Gripping the damp cloth tightly over her mouth, she raced for the door, knowing that it would be only seconds before the smoke would overwhelm her. Glass popped and cracked behind her, mimicking the sound of gunshots, but she kept her focus, telling herself that fresh air was just beyond the door.

But when she reached the exit, she found it closed. Yanking on the handle, she realized with horror that it was locked and she was trapped. With the bar's back exit blocked by the fire, this was her only chance of escape.

She shot at the lock, but to no avail. The door wouldn't move. In a blind panic, she started to shout and yell for help, desperately hoping that someone would hear her cries.

The killer had deliberately imprisoned her, shutting her in a place that he obviously hoped would become her tomb.

Ryan raced into town, siren blaring. He'd received a radio call just five minutes previously from emergency dispatch, letting him know that a fire crew and ambulance were on their way to the Starlight Bar in Bethesda. When he'd learned who'd placed the call, his veins had turned to ice—the reply to his question had been "Kitty Linklater."

By the time he arrived at the bar, many of the townsfolk had gathered to watch the place go up in flames, some of them in their nightclothes and slippers. He also saw two paramedics standing by their vehicle. He saw no sign of Kitty.

"Shane!" Ryan shouted, jumping from his truck and seeing his deputy talking to Frank Price. "Where's Kitty?"

"I don't know, boss," he replied, coming over. "Her dad's old pickup truck is here so I'm guessing she's somewhere close by. The fire crew has been delayed by a fallen tree on the highway and we've received orders not to go inside until they arrive."

Ryan looked at the wooden building, where flames were rising majestically from the roof. The large Starlight Bar sign had been burned on one edge and was now hanging by just one corner. As Ryan watched, it came crashing down onto the concrete below, splintering apart.

He ushered the bystanders away, yelling, "This is a dangerous place right now. Stand well back."

He then approached the paramedics, who were standing by their vehicle in the corner of the lot.

"I'm going in," he said. "Somebody might be trapped inside, so please be on standby with oxygen."

One of the paramedics eyed the fierce blaze with concern. "You should wait for the fire crew, sir. It's not worth the risk."

"Oh, it's worth the risk alright," he replied,

turning to Nancy, who was watching the fire and shaking her head. "Can I have that?" he asked, pointing to the scarf she had wound around her neck to ward off the cold. "But I may need to tear it."

Nancy quickly pulled off the accessory. "Take it. Do whatever you need to."

Ryan gripped the scarf and ripped it right down the middle, before taking the pieces to his truck, dropping them to the ground and thoroughly wetting them with water from a bottle.

Shane picked up one of the makeshift masks.

"I kind of guessed you'd want to come inside with me, Shane, but you're under no obligation," Ryan said. "It goes well beyond your normal duties as a deputy and I'd respect any decision to remain outside."

"Are you kidding me?" Shane replied, tying the bandanna over this nose and mouth. "I'm there already." He picked up an ax from the ground. "I brought this from the station. I thought we could use it."

"Great idea. Let's go."

They approached the entrance, closed off with a padlocked chain securing the double doors from the outside. Ryan stood back to allow Shane to hack at the chain with his ax. A few swift blows saw the doors bang open, and a wall of smoke hit them full in the face.

"We go in low," Ryan said, dropping to his knees. "If you think you'll be overcome, get out immediately."

After a thumbs-up from Shane, Ryan began to crawl inside, feeling his way along the warm wood, hearing smashing noises coming from the bar—bottles and bar glasses shattering in the heat. Kitty could be anywhere in this building. He didn't have a clue where to start, and his eyes and throat were already burning from the thick acrid smoke. He was functioning on a wing and a prayer, hoping that he would somehow be able to sense her presence and that he would find her alive. He filled his lungs with as much smoke-laden air as he dared and lifted his mask.

"Kitty!" he bellowed into the gloom. "Where are you?"

Kitty was slumped on the floor of the men's bathroom, unable to see much in the smoky blackness. She had managed to wedge some towels beneath the door to slow the intrusion of smoke, but without any windows in this little room, she was completed trapped, knowing that her only hope was rescue. Where was the fire department? She had assumed they would have reached the bar by now. She reckoned she had another five minutes before she passed out, another five minutes of terror before she slipped into a blissful unconsciousness. Her mind drifted in and out of lucidity and she thought she heard voices, someone calling her name.

Then she realized that somebody *was* calling her name.

"I'm here, I'm here!" she yelled between coughs, pulling the towels from the cracks beneath the door.

Seeing Ryan's face appear in the doorway filled her with a joy that she'd never known before. His nose and mouth were covered by a red cloth, dirty with soot, and the whites of his eyes were stark against the grime of his skin. He hauled her into his arms and held her tightly, but only for a second, because they had no time to lose.

"Go with Shane and he'll show you the way out of here," he said, pulling her to the door. "Is Harvey here, too?"

"He's dead on the floor of the bar," she said. "You'll never get him outside."

"I can try," he said, giving her a gentle push toward Shane. "Go! And stay low."

Kitty grabbed hold of Shane's jacket and crawled, allowing him to take the lead. She lost all sense of direction in the smoke and put her faith in Shane's hands. However, she couldn't help but worry about Ryan, risking his life to bring out the body of a dead man. He wasn't prepared to leave anyone behind, dead or alive. It made her realize how honorable he was.

Crawling out into the freshness of the night was like drinking a long, cool glass of water. She gulped the air into her lungs, coughing and spluttering, collapsing onto the parking lot. A paramedic appeared at her side, attaching a mask, helping her onto a gurney and speaking soothing words. Shane sat on the tailgate of the ambulance, gasping for breath, having oxygen administered by a second paramedic.

"Where's Ryan?" Kitty asked from behind the mask. "Is he out?"

The paramedic looked around. "Did the other man come out yet?" she called to the crowd. "Do any of you see him?"

The many people around them shook their heads.

"I have to find him," Kitty said, removing her mask. "I can't leave him."

"No, honey," the paramedic said, pushing her back down onto the gurney. "You're in no shape to go anywhere."

"Please," Kitty begged. "Please let me try."

"He's here!" a voice cried out. It was Nancy. "I see him." Then her voice changed to one of horror. "Is he carrying Harvey? Oh my, is Harvey dead?"

The paramedic treating Kitty firmly repositioned her mask, saying, "It's important that you don't go anywhere, okay?" She then called over to her colleague. "I think this lady's hypoxemic, Steve. Keep a close eye on her while I see to the others."

Then the paramedic rushed toward Ryan and Harvey, checking the dead man's pulse and shaking her head. Nancy and Paul both took off their coats and laid them over the body, kneeling by his side and clasping their hands in prayer. Meanwhile Ryan was doubled up on all fours, coughing and spitting onto the ground, his chest heaving for air.

Kitty lifted her mask and swung her legs over the gurney. Ryan needed her mask, needed her oxygen. Standing up, she tried to call his name, but could manage only a croak. Then her legs gave way beneath her and she hit the ground just as dimness closed in.

Ryan sat in the corridor of Southwestern Hospital, waiting for Kitty to regain consciousness. He had been praying for her while he waited. Finally, he heard Kitty's voice ring out loud and clear. And she wasn't happy.

"I want to go home," she was saying. "I have important things to do."

"You inhaled a lot of smoke, Miss Linklater," the doctor said. "As a precaution, I think we should monitor you for a few more hours. It's already 2:00 a.m., so you might as well stay the night."

Ryan rose from his seat in the hallway and walked to the open door of her room. Only family was permitted in her room while she was unconscious, but she could accept visitors now that she was awake.

"Ryan," Kitty said, clearly pleased to see him. "Will you tell the doctor that I'm okay to go home? I'm fine now."

Ryan shrugged, letting the doctor know that neither of them had any authority where Kitty was concerned. She had clearly already made up her mind.

"I can't prevent you from discharging yourself, Miss Linklater," the doctor said, writing on her chart. "But will you at least assure me that you won't be alone for the next twenty-four hours? Will someone be staying with you?"

"She won't be alone," Ryan said. "I'll be with her."

"Well, okay then," the doctor replied, clicking her pen and facing him. "Bring her straight back in if she experiences any shortness of breath, dizziness or pain."

"Sure thing, Doc."

The doctor eyed Ryan's blackened uniform

and his grimy face. "The same goes for you," she said. "Keep an eye on each other, okay?"

As soon as they were alone in the room, Ryan sat by Kitty's bedside, waiting for her to speak first.

"I expect you have a lot of questions," she said finally.

"Yes, I do."

"The first thing you have to realize is that Harvey was murdered."

"We don't know that yet. Early indications point toward suicide."

She let out a noise of exasperation. "Trust me—he was murdered."

"A suicide note was found in Harvey's car."

"It was planted there."

"Don't you want to know what it said?"

"I don't need to know what it said. It's fake."

Ryan rubbed a hand down his face. There was so much he didn't know, and he needed Kitty's total honesty, so he tried to avoid confrontation.

"I was worried about you, Kitty. Whatever you were trying to do, I could've helped you."

"I needed to handle it by myself," she said. "Harvey promised to give me the CCTV footage from the night of the murder, but only if I went there alone. He also knew the true identity of Molly's killer, but that information has now died with him."

This all sounded a little far-fetched. "He said he knew Molly's real killer?"

"He told me so on the phone this evening."

"You guessed Harvey was the anonymous informant before you talked to him tonight, didn't you?" he asked.

"Yes."

"And you called him in secret after you went to bed?"

"Yes." She rubbed at her temples with her index fingers. "I wish I'd recorded the conversation on my cell phone. I was so focused on pursuing the new lead that I didn't take the time to plan and prepare."

"Can you tell me what Harvey said?"

She hesitated, seemingly unwilling to divulge the details.

"I promise to keep an open mind, Kitty," he said. "I promise."

"I think we already established that you're incapable of keeping an open mind when it comes to my father. You can't even tell the difference between my dad and the guy that killed your sister. Whatever you say and whatever you do, you'll always come back to the same conclusion. In your eyes, my father is a murderer and always will be."

What could he say to that? It was true. And he didn't truly see the need for that to change. A fair, honest jury had convicted Harry Linklater, based on the facts of the case. It wasn't wrong or unfair to view him as a murderer when that's what the state of Oklahoma had decided. But there was one point where Ryan felt he needed to make a change.

"You're right, Kitty," he admitted. "I have a hard time separating your father and Cody Jones. I kind of see them as one and the same person, and that's not right or fair. Your father didn't kill my sister and I'd like to ask you to help me remember that from now on." He held up his hand. "I'm not saying that I believe your father is innocent, but I want to be more impartial and listen to what you have to say without rushing to judgment. How does that sound?"

She smiled cautiously. "It sounds like a good start."

"So do you feel a little more comfortable telling me about your conversation with Harvey?"

"Sure, but remember your promise, okay?"

"I'll remember."

He listened, without interrupting, as she told him the details. Apparently, Harvey had owned up to lying to the police, admitted he had been protecting Molly's real killer and confessed to an unnamed historic crime that was being used to guarantee his continued silence.

"Wow," Ryan said when she'd finished. "That's a lot to take in."

"I know," she replied, swinging her legs over the side of the bed and leaning closer to him. "Somebody was knocking on the door of the bar while I was on the phone with Harvey and I figure it must've been the killer, who overheard our conversation and realized what Harvey was about to do. So he murdered him, took the memory stick, torched the bar, and waited for me to arrive in order to lock me inside and kill me, too."

Ryan took his time to respond. A suicide note had been found in Harvey's car, in which he'd said he was bankrupt, about to lose his business to his creditors and that he was unable to face life without the bar that he'd owned for almost forty years. On the surface, it looked like instead of accepting the situation, he'd set fire to the building and taken his own life. The bullet that killed him almost certainly came from his own gun, and Ryan had seen no defensive wounds on Harvey when he'd laid him out on the parking lot. None of what Kitty was saying matched the evidence, but she clearly wasn't making it up.

"I just want to be clear about this," he said, choosing his words carefully. "You're absolutely certain of what Harvey said? You don't think you could've misunderstood or misheard him at all?"

"No. I remember the conversation almost word for word."

"And you're sure that it was Harvey you were speaking to?"

"Of course I'm sure," she snapped. "I've known Harvey since I was a little girl. Don't you think that I know his voice?" She narrowed her eyes. "You're looking for alternate explanations, aren't you?"

"It's my job to look for holes in any theory."

"Yeah, well, this theory doesn't have any holes. It's watertight."

Her story was interesting. It was intriguing. It was even plausible. But it most definitely was *not* watertight. Harvey might have been maliciously lying, luring Kitty to the bar so that an assailant could kill her. It was looking more likely that Harry had killed Molly with an accomplice, who was now trying his level best to cover his tracks. Harvey could have been used as a pawn in a very dangerous game, one in which he ended up losing his life.

But could Kitty's story be entirely true? Could her father be innocent, after all? Ryan had promised to keep an open mind, so he forced himself to consider every possibility.

As he pondered these things, Shane entered the room, his face somber and downcast.

"Hey, boss," he said. "I thought I'd find you here. The fire crew has put out the blaze, but they found something inside the building."

"What?"

"Another body."

Ryan jumped to his feet. "Whose body?"

"We don't know yet. It was buried beneath the floor. One of the firefighters found it when the boards gave way and he fell through, right on top of it, apparently."

"Hold up," Ryan said. "Did you say it was under the floor?"

"Yeah."

"So this person didn't die in the fire?"

"Oh no," Shane replied. "This person has been dead a long time."

"How long?"

"I'm guessing at least ten or fifteen years."

Ryan locked eyes with Kitty, and she rose from the bed, slipping her hand into his.

"Things just got really weird," she said. "You should go take a look."

EIGHT

Kitty wrapped her arms around her torso, shivering in the parking lot of the Starlight Bar. Harvey's former business had been reduced to little more than ashes. Only the charred timber frame remained upright, like bones that had been stripped of flesh. On the asphalt next to the fire truck were two body bags, one large, one small, both zipped up tight, awaiting transportation to the morgue.

Several firefighters were carefully inspecting the ruins, seeking the primary source of the blaze. The Bethesda residents had long since returned to their homes, but Kitty was sure this would be the talk of the town in the morning.

"It's total annihilation," she said to Ryan.

"The fire chief said that an accelerant was probably used. Someone wanted to obliterate everything."

"The killer needed to make sure that he destroyed any evidence linking him to Molly's murder," she said. "If Harvey kept the CCTV footage from that night, who knows what else he kept?"

"Okay," Ryan said, turning to her. "There are two possible theories here. The first is that Harvey set the fire himself and then committed suicide. The second theory involves Harvey being murdered and his killer torching the bar afterward."

"It has to be the second one," she said. "How did I get locked inside? Somebody else was here."

Ryan rubbed at his chin deep in thought, and she remembered how grateful she'd been to see his face appear in the doorway of the bathroom. If only he would now believe her, she could let down her defenses and truly trust him. They would finally be able to work as a team.

"Yes, somebody else was here," he said after a long pause. "And Harvey was murdered. I believe you, Kitty."

She smiled, throwing her arms around his neck and hugging him. "I've waited forever to hear you say that."

He gently peeled her arms away. "I don't want you to get your hopes up. I'm still not ready to fully accept that your father is innocent."

She took a step back. "You're kidding."

He raked a hand through his hair, its vibrant

red color hidden beneath the sooty layer. "This case is really complicated," he said. "Who knows how your dad might have been mixed up in it?"

"He wasn't mixed up in it. He was framed."

"Without being able to interview Harvey, I have no way of establishing these facts for myself."

"You have *me*," she protested. "I'm a witness to what Harvey said."

He grasped her by the shoulders. "And I believe you're being honest with me, but I can't be sure you have all the facts. Harvey might not have been telling the whole truth, and now that he's gone, we have to try and piece together the clues for ourselves."

"You said you'd keep an open mind. So surely you must accept that my father *might* be innocent?"

"Yes," Ryan replied. "I accept that he might be innocent."

She beamed. "That's a step in the right direction at least. Thank you."

A large hearse pulled into the lot, rolling to a stop next to the body bags on the ground.

Ryan held Kitty's hand, lacing his fingers through hers. "You okay to do this?"

She nodded, and together they walked to greet the men exiting the black hearse, which bore the State of Oklahoma Medical Examiner logo.

"Hey there, guys," Ryan said, shaking the hands of the uniformed men, clearly familiar with both. "We're wondering if we could take a look at one of the bodies here."

The older man unloaded a gurney from the back of the vehicle. "Sure thing, Lawrence." He glanced at Kitty. "Is she allowed to look, too?"

"She's a potential witness to a crime that occurred here this evening so I'm giving her special permission to view the remains. One of these bodies belongs to Harvey Flynn and the other is unknown. We'd like to take a look at the unknown."

"Let me check the tags," the man said, bending to read the labels attached to the zippers. "Okay, this is the one you want—found under the floor, right? We'll lift it onto a gurney."

As the two men each took an end of the bag, they both expressed surprise at the weight of the person inside.

"Whoa," the younger one said. "This feels like just bones."

"Let's take a look," his colleague said, unzipping the bag and revealing the head inside.

Kitty put a hand over her mouth and gasped as a skull came into view, dry and white, seeming almost as unreal as a Halloween prop. She felt Ryan's arm slide around her shoulder and pull her close.

"How long would you say this person has been dead?" Ryan asked.

The young man sucked air through his teeth. "It's impossible to say for sure without doing some tests. I'd estimate at least ten or twelve years, but possibly as many as twenty."

"Will you be able to tell the cause of death?" Kitty asked.

"I can take a good guess just by looking at the head," the older man interjected, pointing to a large crack in the white dome. "There's a skull fracture right there."

Kitty swallowed away a sudden feeling of sickness. Who was this tragic person? And how had he or she ended up here? Many of Bethesda's residents had spent evenings in the bar, never knowing they were just a few feet away from a decomposing body. It was a horrifying thought.

Ryan read her mind. "How did people in the bar not notice the odor? The smell of a dead body is hard to hide."

The man shrugged. "Who knows? Maybe the owner closed the bar for a while. Maybe he said that a possum died in the crawl space underneath. That happened in my house one time and it stunk up the place. Nobody would assume that a human corpse was under the floor, right?"

Kitty shook her head. "We'd never have suspected Harvey of anything like that."

The man zipped up the bag. "We all done?"

"Yeah, thanks," Ryan said. "I appreciate your help."

Kitty watched the two bodies being loaded into the hearse and driven away for autopsy. All the while, Ryan's arm remained around her shoulder, squeezing her reassuringly.

"Do you have any idea who that person might be?" he asked.

"None at all, but Harvey said he did a bad thing many years ago. That must've been what he was talking about." She turned to him. "He murdered someone and buried the body under the floor of his bar, and he got away with it."

Ryan looked into the distance where the hearse was disappearing off down Main Street. "I think he paid a high price in the end."

"Can we go home now?" she asked. "I really need to rest."

"Sure," he said, bringing her in close for a hug. "I'll keep watch while you sleep."

Ryan stood on the porch deck, coffee in hand, listening to the Canada geese honking over the lake. Kitty had been asleep for almost four hours and he was keeping guard, running on little more than coffee and adrenaline. He simply didn't know what to make of this latest news. Kitty fervently believed that Harvey had been protecting the real killer of Molly Thomas, but Ryan was determined to give the matter thoughtful consideration before arriving at a conclusion. Harry Linklater had been convicted by a jury on clear evidence. He couldn't just ignore that fact, no matter what protest Kitty put up.

"Hi."

He turned around and saw her coming through the door. Wearing jeans and a turtleneck sweater, she appeared thin and drawn, her thick hair tied loosely in a topknot to reveal her slender neck. He wondered if she'd been losing weight through stress.

"It's nice and peaceful out here," she said. "But those Canada geese sure are noisy sometimes."

He gazed across the water. "I like the sound. It's like they're talking to each other."

"Yeah," she laughed. "In a really angry way."

"How are you feeling? Did you get much sleep?"

"I drifted in and out," she said. "But I kept seeing Harvey's face and all that blood on the floor." She shook her head and tendrils of hair fell down to her cheeks, brushing the ultrafine wound made by her attacker's knife. "I'm so mad at Harvey for what he's done but I'm sad he's dead. I just don't know how to feel."

"It's normal to be conflicted in a situation like

this," Ryan said. "You probably want to yell at Harvey but you also want to mourn his passing."

She leaned against the porch railing next to him. "That's exactly it."

"Harvey obviously made some bad choices that eventually caught up with him. I just wish he was still alive to answer some questions. We sure could use a good lead."

"Is there any news on the body that was found under the floor?"

"All we know at the moment is that the bones belong to a young woman and she was wearing a blue homemade dress. The forensics team is doing their best to extract some DNA from a bloodstain on the fabric, but it's degraded over time so it might take a while. In the meantime, I've got Shane trawling through the missing persons records from ten to twenty years back to see if we can get a list of possible names together. Whoever she is, I want to make sure she gets home. It's not right that she's been lying under those dirty floorboards all these years. She deserves a proper and dignified resting place for her family to visit."

He turned his head toward the breeze blowing off the lake in order to dry the moisture in his eyes. The discovery of that woman's body had taken an unexpected toll on him, stirring his sympathies and giving him cause to worry for her family. At least *his* family had been able to bury Gina properly and begin the grieving process. There was a grave to visit where flowers could be laid on the anniversary of her death, and where balloons could be tied on her birthday. He was thankful for that, at least. Gina hadn't been entombed beneath the floor of a seedy bar, wrapped in a filthy sheet and long forgotten.

Kitty rested her palm on his back, right between his shoulder blades, and made small circular movements with the heel of her hand.

"This is hard for you, isn't it?"

He could only nod.

"Has it brought back some memories?"

"Yes, it has," he said, focusing on the smooth, clear water. "But it's also made me realize that there's a family out there who've been waiting years to learn what happened to their daughter or sister or mom. I should be grateful that Gina has a headstone and a plot of her own—that my parents and I were able to get closure." He broke off and glanced skyward. "How crazy does that sound? I'm grateful that my little sister has a grave."

"You're grateful for the small things that keep you going in grief," Kitty said. "That's how we all get through tough times."

"For a long time, I assumed that God had

abandoned us. That's why I joined the sheriff's department. I thought that if God couldn't keep people safe, then I'd have to do it on my own."

"And do you still feel that way?" she asked.

"Sometimes," he admitted. "I have good days and bad days. I still believe in keeping people safe—it's why it's always been my dream to be sheriff, the one in charge of protecting the whole community. But it's harder than I thought it would be when I was a kid, to know what to do."

She continued to rub his back, her closeness giving him goose bumps.

"'And the light shineth in darkness; and the darkness comprehended it not,'" she said. "That's what you told me, wasn't it?"

"Those are the words we had etched onto Gina's headstone," he said. "It reminds me that she's surrounded by light and nothing can hurt her now. She's in perfect peace."

"Tell me about her," Kitty said. "If you feel ready."

He usually hated to talk about Gina, preferring to keep her memory locked tightly away. But Kitty's gentle voice coaxed him and he found himself speaking freely without even trying.

"My sister was a strong girl," he said. "She was so independent and never let anybody help her prepare for school in the morning. Then she broke her collarbone falling from her bike and she pestered me to braid her hair every day because she couldn't lift her arms to do it herself. Our mother offered to help, but Gina insisted that I do it. She said my braids were the best in school." He laughed. "I was teased a lot about that but I didn't mind. I could never refuse Gina anything."

Kitty laughed, too. "I never had you pegged as a man who could braid hair."

"And you'd be right," he said. "To tell you the truth, my braids were terrible and had always fallen out by the recess bell, but Gina never cared. She used to tear around the schoolyard with her hair flying behind her, pretending to be a superhero. She really was something else."

"She sounds like a cool kid."

"She could've been anything she wanted," Ryan said, finding the words coming quickly and easily. "Even in kindergarten it was clear that she was really intelligent. She wanted to be a doctor or a lunch lady." He laughed again. "She said that both jobs helped children to stay healthy, so there was some logic to her choices."

He wiped away a tear that had leaked from his eye, but it hadn't sprung from a place of sadness. For the first time ever, he was reminiscing with joy, remembering Gina's oddities and quirks, the things that had made him love her, the things that made him *still* love her.

"Thank you," he said quietly.

"For what?"

"For listening."

"Anytime."

He rotated to face her. "I'm sorry if I've been hard on you these last few days. You knew something wasn't right about Harvey's testimony and nobody believed you, not even me. I should've been more willing to listen. I let you down."

She leaned in close. "No, you didn't let me down. You've kept me safe since you got here to Bethesda. We've had a difference of opinion, that's all." Her breath was warm on his lips, her mouth perilously close. "But now that we're both on the same page, things can be different."

He pulled away. "No, Kitty, we're not on the same page. There's a lot of investigating to do before we can get to the truth."

Her face grew pained, and his heart heaved with regret.

"I thought you'd realize the truth after you'd had time to think about it," she whispered.

"I need lots more time to look into things before I know where I stand," he said. "What you're asking is huge. You're expecting me to throw my support behind a convicted murderer without even being sure of the facts."

"Okay," she said, backing away from him. "I understand. I'll leave you to think."

"Please, Kitty," he said, holding an arm out to her. "Just because we don't agree on this doesn't mean we can't be friends. I'm enjoying being with you right now."

"I can't," she said, continuing to back away. "I want you to be someone you're not, and it hurts. I'd like to be by myself for a while. If I need you, I'll let you know."

"What about me?" he said. "What if *I* need *you*?"

"You don't need me," she said, going back inside. "You never needed me."

Kitty sat on her bed and dried her eyes before going downstairs and facing Ryan again. She was embarrassed, hurt and sad, and she didn't want him to see any of that raw emotion.

"Don't look at me like that, Shadow," she said to the cat sitting at her feet. "I never wanted to end up caring about him."

Shadow meowed and headbutted her ankles as if understanding she was in turmoil, and she reached town to tickle his chin.

How had this happened? She'd been doing okay by herself, relying on nobody and retreating into solitude at her lakeside home. Her feelings for Ryan had developed outside her control and now she didn't know what to do with them. There was no way she would allow herself to grow even closer to a man who didn't support her fight to free her father.

There was a knock at the front door downstairs and Ryan opened up. Deputy Harmon's voice filled the hallway and the two men began talking. She heard the words *murder*, *missing* and *pattern*.

"Kitty!" Ryan was calling her. "We could really use your help down here."

"I'll be there in a second," she called back, fanning her eyes with her fingers.

She stood, took a deep breath, ran a brush through her hair, slicked on some lip gloss and dabbed a little scent on her wrists.

"Oh, will you stop looking at me like that?" she said to Shadow. "I'm not doing this for *his* benefit."

She found Ryan and Shane in the kitchen, sitting at the table, where seven photographs were spread across the pine top. Each one showed a young blonde woman, some of them smiling for the camera, some expressionless police mug shots. But their features were spookily similar, as if they could be family relations.

Ryan put a hand on Kitty's shoulder and steered her out of the kitchen, back into the hallway, standing close and leaning in.

"Please don't shut me out, Kitty," he whispered. "I never meant to hurt your feelings."

She shrugged. "I'm not blaming you. It is what it is."

"What you said out there on the porch isn't true. I *do* need you." He put his other hand on her waist. "I'm only just now realizing how much."

She lifted her face so that it was only an inch or so from his. "It doesn't matter, Ryan," she said. "Ever since the guilty verdict was announced, I've been desperately hoping that someone, *anyone*, would listen to me and believe me when I say that justice hasn't been served. Even the townsfolk who've been kind to me think I'm on a wild-goose chase. They don't call me crazy to my face, but I know they think it. I've spent a year dreaming that one day somebody would hold me close and tell me I'm right and have nothing to be ashamed of. All I ever wanted was for someone to love me for who I am. I want someone who will choose to love me because I'm my father's daughter, not in spite of it."

She bit the inside of her cheek, focusing on the physical discomfort. She would not cry again.

"Can't we try and find a way around this?" Ryan asked.

"There is no way around it," she said. "As soon as we catch this attacker, you should move out. I need to focus on my campaign to free my father, without distraction."

Shane's voice rang out from the kitchen. "Are you two lovebirds done yet?"

"Let's go," she said, stepping away from him. "It sounds like we have work to do."

She entered the kitchen and sat at the table, giving her full attention to the color photographs spread across it. Ryan joined her, choosing the seat the farthest away.

"Okay, Shane," Ryan said. "Tell us what you've found out."

"I've been looking through the missing persons records like you asked," Shane said. "And I found something interesting. During the last fifteen years, these seven young women have all been reported missing in Comanche County. Some of them were in trouble with the law and some were persistent runaways in the past. One of them turned up dead a couple years back, found drowned in a river with her hands tied, but nobody was ever arrested for her murder. Take a good look at them and tell me what you see."

"They all look the same," Kitty said, sliding one of the pictures across the table. The face of a pretty young woman smiled back at her, the sun shining on her back and streaming through her hair. She looked happy and wholesome, as if she didn't have a care in the world.

"But there's something else that's weird—they all look like Molly."

"Bingo!" Shane said, producing an eighth photo from his file: Molly's.

He placed the picture alongside the others, and the similarities were clear to see. All eight girls were blonde and blue-eyed, pale skinned and freckled, with the same slim, long-limbed frame.

"This is no coincidence," Ryan said. "How come this hasn't been flagged before?"

"Only one body was found, and apart from Molly, these girls all have troubled histories," Shane replied. "They're the type of people that are likely to skip town, so the police never really looked into their disappearances very closely, especially as they vanished about two years apart. There are hundreds of missing people in Oklahoma alone, so difficult cases like these don't get much attention."

"You know what this could mean, don't you, Shane?" Ryan asked.

"Yes, sir. We might have a serial killer on our hands."

Kitty gasped. "A serial killer."

"It's a possibility," Shane said. "Repeat killers will often target the same type of person because they're obsessed with a particular physical characteristic."

"And do you think that this serial killer also murdered Molly?" Kitty asked.

"It seems likely," Shane said. "The killer obviously didn't have time to hide Molly's body like he did with the others, so he tried to burn it instead. Maybe he acted on impulse when he attacked her and didn't take the time to plan. He got sloppy."

"Which is why he asked Harvey for help," Kitty said. "He was caught in the open and needed a safe place to clean up."

"I think that the body under the floor of the Starlight Bar might be a victim of the same killer, too," Shane said. "Chances are she was young, blonde and blue-eyed." He waved a hand over the pictures. "She might even be one of these."

"And Harvey possibly hid the body in exchange for cash," Kitty said, her voice rising with the realization that they were putting all the pieces together. "He told me on the phone that he'd been young and stupid and he'd needed the money, so somebody could've paid him to help dispose of the body."

"It all adds up," Shane said, looking at Ryan. "What do you think, boss?"

"I agree," he said. "I think we're onto something big."

"So you both accept that my father didn't murder Molly?" Kitty asked hopefully. "If she was murdered by a serial killer who's still on the loose, then my dad's innocent, right?"

The glance exchanged between Ryan and Shane was impossible to read. They were silently communicating, and she didn't like the vibes.

"What?" she asked. "It all adds up. You just said so."

"Molly's blood was in your dad's car, Kitty," Ryan said. "That's a red flag right there."

"I already explained how that got there," she protested. "Molly had fallen while walking to the party. She'd cut her knees."

Ryan wouldn't meet her gaze. "We have to consider the possibility that your father was somehow involved in the murder that night. A victim's blood in a vehicle is usually a dead giveaway. Especially when even your father admitted he was the last person known to have seen her alive."

"He's right, Kitty," Shane said gently. "Nobody saw Molly fall and hurt herself, and it all seems a little too convenient that she was already bleeding when your father gave her a ride. Perhaps your dad didn't administer the fatal blow, but it's likely that he was an accomplice at the very least."

"You're wrong," she said. "I can't believe you're now accusing my dad of multiple murders."

"Serial killers can sometimes work in pairs," Shane said. "We should look at your father's whereabouts when these girls went missing and see if we can spot a pattern."

Kitty stood so abruptly that her chair clattered to the floor. "This is ridiculous!" she shouted. "My father is not a serial killer, and I refuse to listen to this garbage anymore."

She stalked into the hallway, ignoring Ryan calling her back. Instead, she raced upstairs and into her room, where she threw herself onto the bed, buried her face in a pillow, and let out a deep and unrestrained scream.

Ryan stood in front of the television, watching the news correspondent on the screen. The somber-faced woman was reporting outside the ruins of the Starlight Bar, giving details on the apparent suicide of Harvey Flynn and the discovery of a decomposed body beneath the floorboards of his property.

"The fifty-eight-year-old bar owner was a well-known member of the Bethesda community," the reporter said to the camera. "So just what prompted him to take his own life last night? And who exactly is the mystery person that has been buried underneath his floor for many years? Anybody with information regarding this matter should contact Sheriff Jim Wilkins in Lawton."

Ryan switched off the TV with a sigh. Harvey's death was being widely reported as suicide, but he knew different. Somebody out there had murdered Harvey to prevent him from revealing the man's involvement in Molly's death. The one person who might be able to shed some light on the matter was Harry Linklater. But he had been maintaining his innocence since day one and would be unlikely to change his story at this stage. And, Ryan told himself, Harry just might be telling the truth about his innocence. Just about anything was possible.

A creak in the hallway alerted him to movement. He grabbed for his gun in its holster and Kitty's voice floated through the air.

"It's okay, Ryan. It's only me. I'm getting a glass of water."

He walked through to the kitchen to see her fill a glass with mineral water, add some ice and lemon, and take a sip. She padded across the linoleum floor in her socks, taking a bag of chips from a cupboard and putting it in the pocket of her sweatshirt.

"You hungry?" he asked. "You didn't have any dinner."

"I just want a snack. I'll take it to my room."

"Can we talk first?"

She placed the icy water on the counter and ran her finger up and down the condensation on the glass. "Is there anything left to say?"

He could think of a million things, but he knew she wasn't in the mood to hear them. The suggestion that her father might be one-half of a serial-killing duo had hit hard.

"There's a church service tomorrow to remember Harvey. I'll be going along at 10:00 a.m. I wondered if you wanted to come with me."

"There's a service to remember Harvey? Really? After everything he's done?"

"The townsfolk don't know the full story," he said. "None of us do, really. We can't say for sure how that woman came to be buried beneath the floor of the bar, and the pastor decided it would be a nice gesture to say prayers for both Harvey and the unknown woman. It might help the town to heal."

She looked down at her feet. "You're right. I'd like to come if you think it's safe."

"I'll be with you the whole time, and it's a very public place, so there's very little risk."

"Okay."

They stood in silence for long moments. Ryan

enjoyed spending quiet time with her, liked the hush of nighttime by the lake and wished he wouldn't have to leave this place. It already felt like home.

"I'd like to go and see my dad soon," she said. "He considered Harvey a good friend for many years, so he'll be emotional I'm sure."

"I have some time on Monday afternoon if that's good for you?"

"Sure."

Their conversation was horribly stilted and awkward, and he hated sensing Kitty pulling away from him.

"Perhaps you'd reconsider coming inside the prison this time," she said.

"And meeting your father?"

"Yes."

Remembering his promise to keep an open mind, he gave the question the consideration it deserved. He imagined himself sitting at a table with the convicted killer. Try as he might, he couldn't conjure up Harry's face. Every time he envisaged being at that table, he saw the face of Cody Jones in front of him.

"I'm not sure I can do that, Kitty," he said.

She held his gaze for a long time. "I figured you'd say that."

"I want to try and help you. I really do."

In this low light, she appeared little more than

a silhouette as she turned, picked up her glass and shook her head.

"Well, stop trying, Ryan," she said, walking away. "Because you're just making it worse."

NINE

Kitty pushed open the gate that led to the pretty white church. This was the first time in over a year she had attended a church service in Bethesda and she was nervous about stepping inside.

She used to attend with her father after her mother died, but gradually, as her dad's drinking increased, she'd found it more and more difficult to drag him out of bed on Sunday mornings. So she went alone, sidestepping people's questions about her father's health. Kitty had not set foot in a church since her father's conviction, too full of sorrow at the unfairness of it all.

Would God welcome her back? she wondered. She had raged at Him for a long time, blamed Him for her troubles, pushed her Bible aside and retreated into her grief. But recently she felt herself opening up to the joys of faith again, and Ryan had a lot to do with it. His own struggle with faith reassured her that she was normal, that God would forgive her disobedience.

Ryan took her hand and squeezed it, and despite her best intentions, she squeezed back. She hated herself for needing him and wished she could simply switch off the complex feelings she had developed. He could not offer her what she wanted, and she would be a fool to pretend otherwise.

"I'm not sure I can do this," she said, stopping in her tracks on the path. "What if nobody wants me here?"

"Don't be silly," Ryan replied. "The pastor said everyone was welcome to attend this memorial service, and that includes you."

But he barely got the words out before someone else piped up, saying, "You've got a lot of nerve coming here today, missy."

"Oh no," Kitty said, squeezing her eyes tightly shut. "Frank Price."

"Now is not the time or the place, Frank," Ryan said, putting his arm around Kitty. "Show some respect."

"That's exactly what I'm doing," he said, walking up the path with Sheila on one side and Buzz on the other. "I'm showing respect for a dead man. Kitty can show her respect by staying away. After all, she never really cared for Harvey."

"That's enough, Frank," Ryan said. "Can't you lay off Kitty, just for one day?"

"It sounds like someone's in love," Frank said nastily, walking on past. "Just because you're sweet on Kitty doesn't mean I have to be nice to her. I'll have my say."

"Be careful, Frank," Ryan called after him. "You don't want to get yourself arrested for harassment now, do you?"

At that moment, Kitty wanted to hug Ryan for being firm with Frank when she felt so vulnerable. Facing the town in its entirety was always tough, and she welcomed someone shielding her.

"I'm so sorry," Sheila said, slowing to a halt and allowing Frank to walk on ahead. "He's in a foul mood this morning, worse than usual, so I'd give him a wide berth if I were you."

Kitty eyed the discolored skin around Sheila's eye, a bruise that her heavy makeup couldn't cover. By the looks of it, Frank's foul mood had already taken a heavy toll on his wife.

"Are you okay?" Ryan asked. "You look like you've got an eye injury."

"Oh, this," she said, gingerly touching the bruise. "I fell against a coffee table."

Ryan reached into his shirt pocket and pulled out a business card. "Take this. If you need me at any time, just call."

Sheila put up her hand. "I don't think that's necessary. I'm fine, really I am."

"Take it, Grandma," Buzz urged. "Quick, before Grandpa turns around."

Sheila's eyes darted to her husband and back to Ryan. She then plucked the card from his fingers, deposited it in her purse and linked her arm through her grandson's without another word.

Buzz smiled at Kitty, and she returned the smile with gratitude. A gesture of kindness, no matter how small, had the power to lift her spirits.

"Do you believe the story about falling on a coffee table?" she said, as soon as Sheila and Buzz were out of earshot.

"Sure, if you switch 'I fell' for 'I was pushed,'" Ryan replied. "She might have hit the coffee table, but Frank was the cause of it. I've heard all the regular excuses before. Some women walk into doors, others slip on floors and one woman even told me that her dog caused her black eye."

Kitty saw Frank stop at the church door, turn around and wait impatiently for his family, foot tapping.

"Sheila's been married to Frank for forty years," Ryan said. "That's a long time to put up with physical abuse. Doesn't anybody in Bethesda ever try to stage an intervention?"

"The Price family is very private," Kitty said, remembering how her father had attempted to reason with Sheila a few years back, when he caught sight of bruises on her upper arms. "Sheila has never admitted there's a problem, and probably never will. But Buzz is growing into a strong young man, and I reckon he'll decide to step in soon enough."

"I'm not sure about Buzz anymore," Ryan said. "He's kind of secretive."

"I've known Buzz since he was a baby," she said. "And he's a good kid."

"I hope you're right, because Sheila needs someone looking out for her." He offered Kitty his crooked elbow. "Are you ready to go inside?"

She linked her arm with his. "No, but let's do it anyway."

"We can wait awhile if you like."

She suddenly felt as if she had nothing to lose, no reason to hold back her emotions.

"Will you reconsider meeting my father on Monday? I really care about you, Ryan, and if you really, truly care about me, you'll at least think about it. Do it for me."

He swallowed hard, sliding his arm from hers and shifting to stand opposite. He was conflicted. She could see it in his face.

"I'll think about it," he said finally. "For you."

Ryan tried to focus his attention on the pastor's tribute to Harvey, but his mind kept drifting to Kitty and her impassioned request. Meeting Harry Linklater was a big deal. He wasn't sure he could trust himself not to make a scene in the prison meeting room, especially if he saw a smirk on Harry's lips, just like the one he'd seen on the face of his sister's unrepentant killer.

He glanced around the packed church. Practically the whole town had turned out to remember Harvey and say a prayer for the unknown woman recovered from the Starlight Bar. The faces of those present appeared worried, no doubt wondering how a body could have been concealed in their little town right under their noses for so long. Everybody wanted answers and they would be looking to Ryan to provide them.

As the service drew to a close, the pastor invited the congregation to kneel and pray for peace to descend on the town of Bethesda. Ryan reached for the floor cushion under his seat, dropping his Bible as he did so. It fell open at Hebrews and his eyes were drawn to a verse in chapter thirteen: *"Remember them that are in bonds, as bound with them; and them which suffer adversity, as being yourselves also in the body."*

He picked up the Bible, closed it and placed it on his chair, having made up his mind in that briefest of moments. He would visit Harry Linklater in prison and he would do it without complaint. He had been reminded that it was his duty to do so.

After the prayer was completed, he looked at Kitty. She had remained in her kneeling position, head bowed, eyes tightly shut. He rose to his feet, giving her the time and space to unburden herself. That's when he saw Sheriff Wilkins heading his way, weaving through the throng of people, his mustache drooping with the downturned corners of his mouth.

"Hello there, Ryan," he said, with a passing glance at Kitty. "Can I speak with you for a moment?"

Reluctantly, he said, "Sure," and led the sheriff to the back of the church, where some members of the congregation were standing and chatting, a handful crying after the emotion of the service. The atmosphere was highly charged, and the sheriff was about to add his own strong feelings to it.

"Can you tell me why Shane has got a ridiculous theory about a serial killer being on the loose?" the sheriff whispered, steering Ryan to a quiet corner. "Please tell me you didn't put the idea in his head."

"I think it might be a little more than a ridiculous theory, Jim," Ryan said. "Did you see the similarities between those young women who've disappeared over the years? They're all dead ringers for Molly Thomas."

"That proves nothing," the sheriff scoffed. "Apart from poor Molly herself and the girl who washed up in the river a couple years back, the others are probably alive and well, started afresh someplace else. You can't go assuming they've all been murdered."

"We should at least investigate it," Ryan argued. "The body found beneath the floor of the Starlight Bar could be a victim of the same killer. And this guy might still be out there, ready to strike again."

The sheriff's bushy blond eyebrows lowered until his pupils were barely visible.

"Even if there has been more than one murder, how do you know it wasn't Harry Linklater behind them all? We know he killed Molly, don't we?" he said through gritted teeth. "Are you seriously saying that you think we put the wrong man in prison?"

"No. I mean maybe. I don't know. Perhaps Harry was involved in her killing somehow, but I strongly suspect there's another man out there who was part of it. He's been attacking Kitty and he killed Harvey to stop the truth from being revealed."

The sheriff put a firm hand on Ryan's shoulder, pressing down hard. He spoke in the quiet manner of a man trying to restrain his anger.

"Some crackpot is angry at Kitty for stirring up trouble, and Harvey set fire to his bar and then took his own life because his business was about to go bankrupt."

"We don't know that's what happened to Harvey for sure, Sheriff."

"That's what the investigation will conclude, Ryan." The sheriff checked the vicinity to ensure they weren't being overheard. "There's no serial killer and there's no danger to the public. If you start spreading news like this, you'll create pandemonium."

"But what if it's true?"

"It's *not* true." The sheriff had raised his voice, causing people to turn and stare. He smiled cordially and lowered his tone again. "I'm ordering you to let this ridiculous idea go, Ryan. Your close relationship with Kitty has affected your judgment and you're looking for ways to prove her father's innocence."

"That's not what I'm trying to do, Jim," Ryan protested. "It really isn't."

"Isn't it? I see you're still living down by the lake. Didn't I ask you to move out of that place?"

"Yes, you did, but it's not fair to ask that of me. Kitty's in real danger. I can't leave her alone right now."

The older man smoothed the strands of his mustache with his thumb and forefinger, breathing so hard that his nose whistled slightly.

"Well, I guess you've made your choice then," he said, putting on his hat and setting it straight. "Next week I'll be announcing my support for Sergeant Stephen Hopper to be our next county sheriff. As you know, he's one of my best men from Lawton. However much as I'd like to see you take over my job when I retire, I can't endorse a man who's so closely tied with the Linklater family. The press would have a field day."

Ryan's belly turned over with disappointment. He knew this news was likely coming, but it devastated him nonetheless. Ever since he was a teenager he'd imagined becoming county sheriff, but the dream was now evaporating. It might be many years before another chance came his way.

"I respect your choice, Jim," Ryan said. "But I have to follow my conscience and do what I think is right."

"So you're prepared to throw away your career on Kitty?"

"I'm keeping her and the community safe. Everything else is irrelevant."

"I admire your resolve, Ryan," the sheriff said, offering a handshake. "Even if I don't understand it."

Ryan watched him weave his way through the crowd, heading for the door. Ryan could run for the office of sheriff without the endorsement of Jim Wilkins, but it would be futile. The sheriff was hugely popular and widely influential. Without his support, Ryan's election hopes were dashed, but he'd learn to accept it in time. Being a chief deputy wasn't such a bad life, and he vowed to count his blessings.

Kitty had now finished her prayer and was rifling through her purse. Ryan suspected that she needed nothing inside, but was avoiding engaging with the people watching her. Some were staring with open hostility and Frank appeared to be their chief cheerleader, as he stood beside Carla, talking loudly about Harvey's "issues with harassment."

Ryan caught Kitty's eye and pointed to the door, motioning to leave. She eagerly zipped up her purse and made her way to him. She was wearing a fawn-colored coat and pink skirt suit, and had spent a long time on her appearance that morning, he knew, clearly wanting to make the right and reverent impression under the circumstances. Her indecision had made her appear insecure and vulnerable, and he had worked hard to reassure her that nobody would judge her on her clothes.

But he'd been wrong.

"I might've known you'd treat this service as a runway show, Kitty," Carla said unpleasantly. "It's always got to be about you, hasn't it?"

"That was mean, Carla," Joe said, stepping away from his wife. "Kitty, I'm glad you came today. It's good to see you."

An elderly couple nodded in agreement and patted Kitty's shoulder as she passed. It was heartwarming to see that her detractors were small in number and often put in their place by the good people of Bethesda.

Ryan held out his hand for her to take, which she did with a tense smile. "Ignore the haters," he said. "You don't need their approval."

"It sometimes feels like I'm fighting a losing battle with some people."

He caught sight of Sheriff Wilkins's big frame slipping out the exit. "You know something, Kitty? I feel the same way."

Kitty could scarcely believe what she was hearing. "You want to meet my father? This isn't a joke, is it?"

"No," Ryan said. "It's not a joke."

She smiled, though she was still suppressing the feeling of rising happiness in case something happened to snatch it away.

"And you're absolutely sure?"

"Yes, I'm absolutely sure."

"What persuaded you?"

"Let's just say I had a change of heart."

She felt both euphoria and anxiety. Did Ryan want to interview her father about the body beneath the floor? Was he using this visit as an opportunity to accuse her dad of being involved with a serial killer?

She walked to the sink to fill the kettle. "Will you be asking him any questions?"

"How do you mean?"

"Is this just a chance to try and pump him for information? You and Shane still think he might be responsible for Molly's murder and maybe even more besides, don't you? So if you're planning on using the visiting time to interrogate him, then I'd rather you didn't come at all." She realized that she sounded defensive so she softened her tone. "It would upset him, you see. And he didn't look well the last time I saw him."

"I won't be questioning him, Kitty," Ryan said. "To be honest with you, I have no idea what I'm going to say. But whether he committed a crime or not shouldn't really matter. He's in prison and he deserves some compassion."

Kitty was taken aback by this. Showing consideration to prisoners had never been high on Ryan's agenda before. In fact, he actively believed that those convicted of a crime should serve their time as a penance. Hadn't he said that murderers deserved no visitors at all?

"What about the man who killed your sister?" she asked. "Should he be shown compassion, too?"

At the question, Ryan's face betrayed an inner struggle and he rubbed the back of his neck while leaning against the kitchen counter, his shirtsleeves rolled up to the elbow.

"Yes," he said. "I guess everybody deserves a second chance, and that includes Cody Jones."

"Wow, Ryan," she said, lifting two mugs from their hooks on the wall. "I never thought I'd hear you say that. It isn't easy to show kindness to someone who's stolen something so precious, and I'm really proud of you for trying."

"If I don't try, I'll never fully move on, right?"

She smiled at him, wondering how she was going to switch off her growing attraction to him now that he was truly opening up, revealing his weaker side and confiding his deepest feelings.

"Hating someone takes a lot of energy," he said. "And I hated my sister's killer with a passion that consumed me for a long time after her death. Jones was all I ever thought about." He threw his hands in the air. "How stupid is that? I wasted countless hours imagining ways I could hurt him. It helped no one, least of all me."

"You're right," she said, moving closer to him,

sliding her hand across the smooth kitchen counter as she went. "Hate is incredibly self-destructive."

"That's why I'm frustrated with some of the residents in Bethesda. They're so busy hating you that they're making the whole town suffer. I'm proud of you, too. I'm proud of the way you've dealt with their animosity and their nasty comments. You're a tough cookie, you know that?"

She blushed a little, unreasonably happy with his praise. She knew this conversation was steering her toward dangerous waters, but she didn't have the power to change course.

"I'm not all that tough, really," she said quietly. "I just do a pretty good job of pretending."

He spoke in hushed tones to match hers. "We all pretend to be someone we're not at times."

She leaned in closer. "Even you?"

"Sure. Shane keeps teasing me about my romantic feelings for you, and I pretend he's got it all wrong. I hide behind my uniform and say it's my job to take care of everyone. But any fool can see that I care for you a whole lot more than I care for anybody else. Shane sees it, Sheriff Wilkins sees it, Frank sees it and I'm pretty sure *you* see it."

Kitty was lost for words. She had sensed a special connection between her and Ryan, but had no idea that his feelings ran as deep as hers.

"I've been trying not to get close to you," she said, her lips just millimeters away from Ryan's. "It's too complicated."

She felt his breath on her mouth, warm and sweet. "Yes, it's complicated," he said. "But not impossible."

His hand touched her cheek, cupping one side of her face, his pinkie finger gently running along the faint line left by the knife, as if he could erase it away.

Then she pressed her lips to his, forgetting why she was fighting against his affections. For a few blissful seconds she melted into his embrace, slipping her hand into his and holding tight. At that moment, he was strong and solid and dependable, and she loved him for it. But it was a fleeting emotion.

"This is wrong," she said, pulling away. "I'll only end up getting hurt in the end." She touched her lips where the feel of his lips still lingered. "I'm sorry, Ryan."

"I won't hurt you, Kitty," he said. "I swear."

"You won't hurt me intentionally—I know that. But what if you never change your mind about my father? What if you meet him tomorrow and decide that he's guilty as charged?"

Kitty had been imagining Ryan becoming her greatest ally and her fiercest supporter, standing by her side throughout her struggle to search for the truth. It was a fantasy that was unlikely to ever come true. And that knowledge caused a physical pain to burn in her chest.

Ryan had no answers to give her beyond a simple statement that floored her.

"I think I'm falling in love with you, Kitty."

"No, no, no," she said, walking away from him and wringing her hands. "Don't say that."

"But it's true."

She folded her arms, rubbing her skin through her silky white blouse. "It doesn't much matter how you feel, because unless you can look me in the eye and tell me that you believe my father is innocent I can never love you in return."

She fixed him with a stare, knowing exactly how he felt, but challenging him to say the words, anyway.

"I can't," he said.

She ran quickly up to her bedroom. Why had she tortured herself like that? Why had she kissed Ryan, knowing that it could lead nowhere? She'd been an idiot.

And now they could never go back to the way they were. Now their friendship was surely over.

"Where's Kitty?" Shane asked, entering the house with a box file in his hands. "My investigation has turned up something interesting."

"She's resting," Ryan said, bolting the door

behind his deputy. "And I don't think she wants to be disturbed."

"I'm okay," she called. "I'll come down. Just give me a second to wash my face."

Ryan looked up the stairs to see Kitty standing at the top, her face blotchy and streaked. He wanted to rush to her side and wrap his arms around her, but his feet were immobile on the floor, fixed there by the sensible voice inside his head telling him to let her be.

"Is she okay?" Shane asked quietly. "Did you two have a fight or something?"

"Not exactly. Our relationship is, um…" He didn't know how to finish the sentence.

"Problematic?" Shane offered helpfully.

"Yeah, something like that."

"Listen, boss," Shane said, shifting his file from one hand to the other. "I know I tease you sometimes about Kitty, but I don't mean any offense. I realize you like her a lot, and if you want to date her then don't worry about what some hotheads in the town will think."

"It's not that easy. Kitty and I have some differences that we can't seem to resolve."

"Ah," Shane said. "Her father."

"Exactly. You know how fiercely she defends him, and she won't even consider that he might've been involved in Molly's murder."

"Well, it turns out that Harry could be telling

the truth about his innocence, after all," Shane said. "We might've been wrong about him all along."

"You're kidding! What did you find out?"

The deputy went into the kitchen and put his file on the table.

"Okay, so when we found Molly's body, her hands had been tied with rope. The same rope was used to tie the hands on the person under the floor of the Starlight Bar. And it's also the same rope that bound the hands of the girl pulled out of the river two years ago. These three murders are all related."

"Are you sure? Can you come to that conclusion based on the rope alone?"

"This rope is really unusual. It's homemade, not store-bought stuff, made from a mix of things like plastic, bark and grass. We didn't focus too heavily on the rope in Molly's murder investigation because we didn't need to use it to figure out a suspect—Molly's phone records with that text she sent took us straight to Harry."

Ryan turned his ear to the hallway, listening for Kitty's arrival. He didn't want her overhearing his next comment.

"Harry could have used the same rope in all these murders," he said. "He might be responsible for all three deaths."

"I already thought of that," Shane said. "So

I did a little digging. The girl who was found in the river went missing on a summer's day in August and her body was recovered less than twenty-four hours later, so there's only a small window for someone to have killed her."

"And why can't it be Harry?"

"Because during that twenty-four-hour window, Harry was sitting in a jail cell on a DUI charge. There's no way he could've killed that girl."

"Okay," Ryan said slowly. "Maybe Harry's accomplice sometimes acted alone."

"Yeah, that's one explanation, but there's another one we should consider."

"And what's that?"

"The possibility that Harry is innocent, after all."

"Do you think he's innocent?"

"I've given it a lot of thought," Shane replied. "And I have to admit that I'm having doubts about the jury's verdict." He sat down heavily, clearly troubled. "I think we all judged Harry harshly because of his past conviction and alcoholism. But what if he's telling the truth and we won't listen?"

"We don't know that for sure," Ryan said. "I think we need to reexamine Molly's murder, go over evidence with a new eye."

Shane put the photographs on the table. "We

also need to start properly investigating these six missing-person cases. If we can locate their bodies, we can look for the same rope and other similarities in the crimes. If we've got a serial killer operating in the county, we've got to put all our resources into finding him. I've been working flat out with door-to-door inquiries and trawling through databases for suspects who match Kitty's attacker, but it's like looking for a needle in a haystack. We need more manpower."

"I agree," Ryan said. "But we won't be getting extra help any time soon. Sheriff Wilkins is none too happy about this serial killer theory. He reckons we'll cause panic in the town if we start talking about it."

"Sheriff Wilkins only cares about retiring on a high," Shane said. "He's got a big party planned, and he doesn't want anything to upset the celebrations." The deputy put his hand on Ryan's shoulder. "I heard that you won't be getting Jim's endorsement for the role of sheriff. I'm really sorry. In my opinion you'd make an excellent one."

"Thank you, Shane," Ryan said. "I appreciate that. But Jim thinks my association with Kitty would be an embarrassment to him, so he won't back me."

"I tell you what's an embarrassment, boss," Shane said. "Stephen Hopper over in Lawton is barely out of diapers and Sheriff Wilkins wants *him* to take over the job." He laughed. "I can't believe that the sheriff didn't consider endorsing me instead."

"Your time will come," Ryan said, sliding the photos back into the file as he heard Kitty's feet on the stairs. "Can we keep this new information about the rope under wraps for now?"

"You don't want to tell Kitty?"

"No, not right now. Let's give it a little more time."

Kitty would seize this new information and use it to continually push Ryan to acknowledge her father's innocence. And he didn't want to do that just yet. He wanted to meet Harry first, before coming to any firm conclusions.

"Hello, Shane," Kitty said a little frostily, entering the kitchen. She was still nursing the hurt Shane had caused by implying that her father might be in league with a serial killer. "You said your investigation turned up something new. What is it?"

"Oh," Shane said, trying to stall for time. "It's nothing."

"It can't be nothing," she said, her deep brown eyes still moist from her tears. "You said it was something interesting."

"Shane discovered that the missing women

all have the same color eyes," Ryan interjected. "All blue."

She folded her arms. "Is that it? We knew this already."

"We did?"

"Yes. We were looking at the photos yesterday and…" Kitty stopped and narrowed her eyes at the window, as if trying to see into the distance. "Who's that by the barn? Did someone else come here with you, Shane?"

"No," the deputy replied. "I came alone."

The two men locked eyes, senses alert. Ryan stood and reached for his weapon, managing to pull the gun from its holster just as the window shattered with a thunderous bang.

He grabbed Kitty, yanked her to the floor and shielded her body with his own.

TEN

Kitty lay awkwardly on the floor, her arm twisted uncomfortably beneath her, but she didn't dare move an inch. The floor was strewn with fragments of glass.

After the initial bang had died away, a silence followed, and all three inhabitants of the house remained crouched on the floor in apprehension.

"What was that?" Kitty whispered.

"A bullet," Ryan replied, pointing at the destroyed clock on the wall close to where Kitty had been standing. "I think he was aiming for your head."

She shifted position to free her twisted arm, but Ryan pushed her back down to the floor.

"Don't move," he said. "He's probably waiting for you to show yourself."

"What do you want to do, boss?" Shane asked. "Should we get Kitty somewhere safe?"

Ryan eyed the door to the cellar. "Kitty, why

don't you lock yourself in the panic room and wait there?"

She didn't really want to be shut away in the dark, unable to assist.

"My gun is in the living room," she said. "I'd rather stay here and keep guard. At least I'll be able to help if you get into trouble."

Ryan didn't look convinced, but Shane reacted in an instant, crawling along the floor toward the living room. "Where's the gun, Kitty? I'll get it for you."

She pushed herself up onto all fours. "It's in the top drawer of the unit in the corner."

As Shane made his way from the kitchen, Ryan raised his head above the sink to peer out. Immediately, a bullet zinged through the broken window and hit the table, sending wood shavings spitting into the air.

"Shane, keep low!" he yelled. "Don't let him see you."

Shane returned on his belly, dragging himself across the floor, gun in hand. He gave it to Kitty, saying, "Don't fire unless you have a clear shot, okay?"

She looked from Ryan to Shane. "Aren't you going to call for backup or something?"

"Backup would have to come all the way from Lawton," Ryan said. "And it would take close to an hour. We don't have that amount of time to waste." He checked the bullets in his gun. "Shane will go out front and I'll go out back, and we'll close in on this guy from both sides. Kitty, you saw him by the barn, right?"

She nodded. "He was under the apple tree next to the barn and he was dressed in camouflage."

"Keep your cell phone close by and holler if you need help," he said. "Remember to stay out of sight. We'll be back soon."

When both men had left the house, Kitty settled herself next to the kitchen table, where she had a good view of the back door. Her heart thudded in her chest as she waited for something to happen.

The first gunshot caused her to jump and bang her head on the corner of the table. She yelped in surprise and pain, wondering whether it was safe to take a look outside. As the shots intensified, she heard shouting. She recognized Ryan's rich, deep voice, ordering someone to lay down a weapon. The hollering grew louder, angry and chaotic.

Kitty crept along the floor toward the broken window and knelt beneath the sink. Then, ever so slowly, she raised her head to see what was happening outside. The bullet that flew past her head came so close that it created a breeze and she screamed, dropping to the floor again and crawling back to her safe place. But the bullets wouldn't stop coming. They pounded the walls around her, creating a cacophony of noise that rattled inside her belly and disoriented her.

She stood and ran into the hallway, intending to gain a better vantage point upstairs, but a pain sliced into her leg, like a bee sting, and she fell to the floor, curling up in a ball. The gunshots gradually ceased until she was aware only of the sound of herself screaming.

"Kitty," Ryan yelled into the house. "Where are you?"

"I'm here."

He appeared at her side, checking her body for wounds, turning her over on the rug.

"My leg," she said. "Something hit my leg."

He picked her up and carried her into the living room, laying her on the sofa and inspecting her right thigh, where blood was trickling.

"A bullet grazed you," he said. "You're fortunate it wasn't an inch or so to the left. It's not serious."

"There was no letup," she said. "The bullets kept on coming and coming."

"The man by the barn was actually nothing more than a dummy dressed in camouflage to fool us. While Shane and I were closing in on it, someone started firing at the house from the cover of the trees. I came back when I heard you screaming. Shane is chasing the guy right now."

"That's not right, making him face this guy alone," she said, pushing herself up to a seated position. "We have to go help him."

Shane's head suddenly appeared at the living room window and he pointed to the lake. "The shooter ran out of bullets and he's getting away in a boat," he shouted. "Kitty, do you keep a boat here?"

She thought of her dad's ancient rowboat, stored upside down in the barn. That wasn't the kind of vessel Shane had in mind. "Not one with an engine," she said. "I'm sorry."

The deputy grimaced and was gone. Then Kitty flopped back onto the sofa and put her hands over her eyes. She heard Ryan go into the kitchen and run the water.

"I can't take this anymore," she said, more to herself than him. "When will it be over?"

"Soon," he said, returning to her side and holding a wet cloth to the bloodstain on her jeans. She winced at the smarting pain.

"We'll get through this, Kitty," he said soothingly. "I promise."

She kept her eyes closed, her hand pressed over them. As much as she wanted to believe his promises, she wasn't sure she could.

Only time would tell.

* * *

Ryan pulled into a parking spot outside the Oklahoma State Penitentiary and turned off the engine. The trip from Bethesda had been quiet. The latest shooting incident at the house had shaken Kitty pretty badly and her small flesh wound was a painful reminder of what might have been. He had floated the idea of canceling their visit today, but Kitty wouldn't hear of it.

She touched his hand, which rested on the wheel. "I telephoned the prison before we left and a guard confirmed that Cody Jones won't be receiving visitors this afternoon, so you don't need to worry about seeing him."

Ryan smiled. She had planned ahead to ease his mind. He was grateful for her thoughtfulness.

"Thank you."

"Remember not to tell my dad about the attacks," she said. "He'll only worry."

"Okay. I'll say nothing."

He stepped from the vehicle first, checking all four corners of the lot to ensure that no danger lurked. When he was certain it was safe, he let Kitty out. With a makeup-free face and long, loose hair, she appeared much younger than her years, but visibly tired.

They approached the prison together in silence. The huge white walls of the penitentiary exuded an aura of menace. Having been here many times before, Kitty led the way, taking him to the correct door, through security and into an open-plan room where numerous chairs and tables were placed, each one inhabited by a man in prison clothes.

Seeing him in person, Ryan finally recognized Harry Linklater from the photograph with the newspaper articles. But he had aged terribly since that time, having developed deep creases in his forehead and lost weight almost to the point of emaciation.

Kitty rushed up to him and hugged him tightly, telling him how well he looked and how she'd missed him. She was falsely bright and cheerful, her smile unnatural.

"Your cut is healing well," Harry said, pointing to her cheek. "You've stopped doing chores in the barn, right?"

She touched the faint line, now faded to a light pink. "I explained to Dad how I cut myself clearing out the barn," she said to Ryan. "And he told me to quit working so hard."

"You should get somebody to do the heavy work for you, Kitty," her father said, eyeing Ryan's build. "This young man looks like he's got muscles enough to help out." He held out his hand. "My name is Harry Linklater, sir, and I'm very pleased to meet you. You must be Ryan

Lawrence. Kitty told me a lot about you on her last visit."

Ryan hesitated, his eyes resting on Harry's bony wrist. Ryan had promised himself that he would never sit at the same table as a convicted child killer, let alone shake his hand. But he had to give this man a chance.

He took the offered hand and shook it. "Your daughter is an incredible woman, Mr. Linklater. You must be very proud of her."

Harry smiled. "Yes, she is, and I don't deserve her at all."

"Oh, Dad, stop it," Kitty said, motioning for them all to sit. "I don't need to hear your apologies again."

"Yes, you do, Kitty," Harry said, his eyes becoming glassy. He gave his attention to Ryan. "I was a terrible father, you see. After Kitty's mother died, I couldn't do a thing except drink, leaving Kitty to handle everything around the house. She cooked and cleaned while I drank my life away. I didn't deserve her then and I sure don't deserve her now."

"It's all in the past, Dad," Kitty said. "Let's forget it."

"Regret is a terrible thing to live with," he said. "I sometimes lie awake at night thinking *what if…*"

"What's done is done," Ryan said, wondering which regrets Harry was referring to. Was murder on that list? "The only way to combat regret is to be truthful about your mistakes and try to atone for them."

Harry nodded in agreement. "You're absolutely right. This time in prison has been the best and worst experience of my life. It's forced me off the booze and given me the opportunity to take a long, hard look at my life."

"And what do you see?" Ryan asked.

"I see a coward and a quitter. I see someone who was selfish and weak, too absorbed in his own sorrow to properly care for his daughter. I see someone that I don't much like—but also someone who's ready to change." He put his hands on the table and laced his fingers together. "I know this might sound crazy, but I feel like a vase that's been broken and glued back together in a way that makes it much stronger."

That didn't sound crazy to Ryan at all. It sounded sensible and humble, and much to his surprise, he found himself asking the question he'd intended to save for much later in the visit.

"Did you kill Molly Thomas?"

He saw Kitty flinch, and Harry closed his eyes slowly as if a pain had shot through him.

"I would never hurt Molly," he said. "She was beautiful both inside and out." Harry looked Ryan square in the eye. "I didn't kill her, but I understand that it's hard to trust a man with a criminal history like mine."

Ryan was glad that Harry brought this up. "You robbed a post office, right?"

Harry took his time in answering. "I did, yes. My parents didn't do a great job in raising me. They cared more about using drugs than about me, and my dad used to knock me around. I was put into my first foster family at the age of ten and everything went downhill from there. I was angry all the time and felt worthless, so I started stealing cars and hanging out with the wrong crowd. I'm ashamed of what I did to those people in the post office and I'd do anything to turn back the clock. After I served my time and met Kitty's mom, she put me on the straight and narrow. She introduced me to God." He smiled. "And she made me see that I wasn't worthless, because I had a Father who loved me. I just wish I hadn't lost sight of Him when she died. I was weak."

"We're all weak sometimes," Ryan said. "We're only human." Harry's words seemed as sincere as they could possibly be, but Ryan needed to hear more from him, more about the night of the murder.

"Tell me what happened when you picked up Molly from the highway," he said.

"It was a Saturday evening and I was driving

to the Starlight Bar. It was rainy and I saw Molly sitting at the side of the road, so I stopped and got out of my truck. She said she was walking to a party at the Sutton farm and she'd fallen over a rock. Her knees were all cut up, so I found some tissues and helped her as best I could. Then I gave her a ride to the party and dropped her at the end of the lane that leads to the Sutton place."

"You didn't take her all the way to the door?"

"She asked me not to." He bowed his head. "She didn't want to say it, but she was embarrassed. She didn't want everyone at the party to see her arriving with me. I understood why—who'd want to be seen getting out of the town drunk's car? And it was only a short walk up the lane." He wrung his hands. "If only I'd insisted on taking her right up to the house, she'd have been safe. I failed her and I'll never forgive myself for it."

Kitty leaned across and put her hand on top of her father's, and he gave her a weak smile.

"Afterward I went on to the bar and stayed there drinking until late, and then I drove home again." He shifted uncomfortably in his chair. "I know it was wrong to drive under the influence, and I deserve to be punished for it, but drunk driving is the worst thing I did that night. The first I knew about Molly's death was when the sheriff arrived at my house the next day with a warrant to take my truck for forensic tests. He said something about probable cause and circumstantial evidence, but I was in total shock. A few days after my vehicle was taken, I got arrested and charged."

Harry's natural answers, his constant eye contact and his straight-talking manner all supported his credibility. Ryan could see why Kitty believed in him so fervently.

"When Molly got out of your car, did you see anybody else around?" he asked. "Or notice anything that might be considered suspicious?"

"No."

"And did you stop anywhere or talk to anybody before going into the Starlight Bar?"

"No."

"And do you know of any reason why Harvey Flynn would refuse to corroborate your alibi?"

"No."

"What about the woman buried beneath the floor of Harvey's bar—do you know anything about that?"

"I'm sorry. I've seen the news about the woman on TV but I have no idea who that dead person is. I'm not much help, am I?"

Ryan rubbed his neck. Harry was apparently clueless, holding no information that would assist his investigation.

"Who else was at the party that night?" he asked. "Surely the police must have interviewed all of them?"

"From what I heard, almost every teenager from Bethesda was there," Kitty interjected. "They all got questioned, but none of them saw or heard anything."

"Was Buzz there?"

"Probably," she replied.

"And did he drive there by himself or did he get dropped off?"

"I don't know." Kitty narrowed her eyes. "Why? What are you thinking?"

"I'm thinking that this might've been an opportunistic killing, by somebody who snatched Molly on the spur of the moment. I don't think it was planned out in advance. How could the killer have known exactly when Molly would arrive? No, I think he acted on impulse. That explains why the body wasn't well hidden. There was no time for him to prepare."

"And you think it might've been Buzz Price?" Harry asked in a low voice.

"I don't think Buzz is our guy," Ryan replied. "But I'm pretty sure he knows more than he lets on."

Harry's expression was suddenly eager. "Does this mean you believe that I didn't do it?"

Ryan turned to Kitty. "Could you get us some

coffee from the machine? I'd like to have a one-to-one with your father."

Kitty looked at her dad, who nodded in agreement, and she rose from her seat to leave them alone.

"I believe you, Mr. Linklater," Ryan said. "And I'm sorry for what's happened. Your daughter never stopped trusting in you and I didn't support her at first. I hurt her feelings and I made her sad by insisting you were guilty, and I'm sorry for that, too. But I promise that I'll work with her to try and figure all this out, because you and Kitty deserve to be taken seriously."

Harry appeared shocked, as if he wasn't expecting such a heartfelt confession.

"Thank you," he said. "I've been so worried about Kitty taking on too much responsibility, and I've been praying that she'd find someone to help her share the load. I can't tell you how happy I am to finally meet the answer to that prayer."

Ryan watched Kitty feed change into the machine, occasionally glancing in their direction, her expression betraying her anxiety about why Ryan wanted to be alone with her father. But Ryan needed to say something personal, something that he didn't want Kitty to hear.

"I like your daughter very much, Mr. Linklater."

"I guessed as much."

"And I wanted to let you know that I'm taking care of her, doing everything in my power to keep her safe."

"Safe?" Harry questioned. "Safe from what?"

He remembered his agreement with Kitty. "It's just a figure of expression. What I mean to say is that she means much more to me than a landlady."

Harry smiled. "You've fallen in love with her."

Ryan's eyes flicked to Kitty.

"I think I have," he said. "And you can be assured that she's in good hands with me."

"I see that. But Kitty is a strong woman and she knows her own mind, so it's not me that you need to persuade. If you love her then go ahead and tell her."

Ryan watched her weave her way among the tables, carrying two plastic cups of steaming coffee, which she set down with a smile.

"So, what have you two boys been talking about?"

"Just the facts of the case," Ryan replied. "I want to get things straight in my head."

The truth of the matter was that he did want to get things straight in his head. He wanted to be sure he could give Kitty the love and support she required before making any declaration of affection.

After everything he had done to hurt her, could he now be the man she deserved?

Kitty sat next to Ryan on the sofa in her living room. Shane was in the kitchen, supervising the repair of the broken window and carefully extracting bullets from the wall for forensic analysis. He'd been there since lunchtime at Ryan's request, and another deputy had been drafted from Lawton to cover the Bethesda station for the afternoon.

Ryan had told Kitty he'd wanted to delay discussing their visit to the prison until they arrived home. He had apparently wanted some time to consider what he was going to say, and she respected his decision. It meant he was taking great care to ensure he took the matter seriously and chose the right words. She appreciated that.

With the sound of a hammer in the background, Ryan took a deep breath.

"I believe that your father is innocent."

Kitty's hands flew to her mouth as a high-pitched squeal pushed its way past her lips. This was the news she had been hoping and praying for.

"I'm so pleased, Ryan," she said. "I just knew you'd change your mind if you met him. He's honest and kind and admits he's done wrong in his life, but you can see he's not a killer." She realized she was rambling, so she forced herself to slow down. "Thank you for giving him a chance."

"I owe you an apology, Kitty," he said. "I allowed my personal situation to cloud my judgment, but if you'll let me make up for it, I'll be the biggest supporter you ever had."

She beamed. This was music to her ears.

"What's in the past doesn't matter anymore," she said, shifting on the sofa to be closer to him. "We're on the same page now and everything looks different."

"I'm glad you said that." He brushed a lock of hair from her cheek. "Because I really care about you, Kitty. You know that, right?"

"Yes."

"Hey, boss!" Shane called from the kitchen. "I need a second pair of eyes on something. You got a minute?"

Ryan jumped up from the sofa. "I'll be right back."

He vanished through the door and Kitty leaned back on the sofa, her legs kicking in the air like a baby on a mat. Despite her continued dangerous personal situation, this day was ranking as perhaps the best in her life so far.

A buzzing sound came from the coffee table and Ryan's cell phone vibrated across the surface.

"Can you get that for me, Kitty?" Ryan called out.

"Chief Deputy Lawrence's cell," she said professionally, after hitting the answer button. "How may I help you?"

"Who's that?"

"My name is Kitty Linklater. Who is this, please?"

"This is Sheriff Wilkins calling from Lawton. What are you doing answering Ryan's cell phone?" The sheriff's voice was gruff.

"Ryan is dealing with something important right now," she said. "Can I take a message?"

"You can tell him to get down to the Bethesda station immediately. Both he and Shane have gone AWOL this afternoon and drafted one of my boys from Lawton to cover. This is unacceptable and I assume *you* are the reason why."

"No, no, it's not like that." She panicked about landing Ryan in trouble. "It's part of an investigation."

"Spare me the excuses, Miss Linklater. I'm fully aware that you and Ryan have got some kind of relationship going on and I've already warned him about the consequences. But if he wants to throw away his chances of becoming sheriff then that's his lookout."

She was confused. "What do you mean?"

The sheriff fell silent for a moment. "I'm guessing he didn't tell you?"

"Tell me what?"

"I told Ryan that I would withdraw my endorsement unless he moved out of your house. He decided not to comply with my wishes so I've chosen another candidate to support."

"You can't do that." She reeled at the unfairness of it all. "Ryan is only trying to do the right thing."

"The right thing would be to focus on the whole community of Bethesda instead of concentrating his resources on the daughter of a convicted murderer. I have a lot of sympathy for you, Miss Linklater, I really do, but you've dragged Ryan into a situation that is tarnishing the reputation of the entire sheriff's department. I hope you realize what you're costing him."

"I—I…" She didn't know what to say or how to defend herself.

"I'd appreciate you letting Ryan know that I called," the sheriff said. "I'll expect to see him at the station in an hour. I'm already on my way."

The line went dead and Kitty stared at the cell for what seemed like an eternity. Ryan had given her no indication of the sheriff's ultimatum. Why hadn't he told her? Was he trying to protect her from the guilt? It didn't really matter, because she refused to be responsible for sabotaging Ryan's career, or keeping him from reaching his lifelong dream.

"All done," Ryan said, reentering the room, wiping dusty hands on his pants. "Who was that on the phone?"

She stood up. "It was Sheriff Wilkins. He wants to see you at the station in an hour."

Ryan checked his watch. "I guess he's a little sore about me stealing one of his deputies this afternoon to man the station. I'll smooth things out with him."

"Why didn't you tell me, Ryan?"

"Tell you what?"

"That the sheriff was no longer endorsing you for the election."

Ryan groaned. "You weren't supposed to find out."

"He says it's because of me."

"Don't listen to what the sheriff says," Ryan said, coming to stand in front of her. He slid an arm around her waist and rested his forehead against hers. "It's not important."

She stepped back. "But it *is* important. You've dreamed of being the county sheriff ever since Gina died. You can't just throw it all away because of me."

"Why not?"

"Because I won't let you."

"I've made my choice, Kitty, and I stand by

it. What's the point in becoming sheriff if I have to sacrifice my relationship with you in order to get the job? I'd be miserable."

"But we don't have a relationship."

"Not yet," he said. "But that could all change." He smiled. "If you want it to."

She wanted to cry with frustration, but she forced herself to remain calm and composed.

"I want the same thing as you," she said. "But if we become a couple I'd always wonder whether you resented me for costing you the sheriff's job."

"I could never resent you."

"You don't know that. You have no idea how you'll feel in the future."

"Yes, I do," he said quietly. "I love you."

She pressed the heels of her hands into her eye sockets so firmly that she saw stars. She needed those few seconds to gather her thoughts and come up with a plan.

"Okay," she said, putting her hands on her hips. "This is what you're going to do—in one hour, you're going to meet with the sheriff at the Bethesda station and you'll tell him that you'll be moving out of this house in the morning. You'll also tell him that you and I are not, and never will be, romantically involved. Then you will ask him to reinstate his endorsement of your candidacy for county sheriff. Got that?"

"No."

"Please, Ryan, don't make this harder than it already is."

"There is no way I'm leaving you in this house all alone. It's madness."

"I have the panic room," she said. "I'll be fine."

Ryan turned around in circles, as if looking for an imaginary path to follow, one that would lead him back to her.

"Won't you at least take some time to think about it?" he asked. "Don't make a rash decision."

"It's not a rash decision," she replied. "It's the right decision. You've worked so hard to get where you are in your career and you *will* be sheriff. I'll expect you to have your bags packed in the morning and I'll try to help you find alternative accommodation."

"You don't have to do this."

"Yes, I do," she said with force. "Things will be different when we prove my father's innocence, but until then, we have to stay apart."

"But, Kitty," he protested. "That investigation could take months or years to conclude. I don't want to wait that long."

"I'm sorry, Ryan," she said, forcing herself to be matter-of-fact. "This is what I want."

In truth, it wasn't what she wanted, not by a

long shot, but what choice did she have? Ryan was being ruled by his heart rather than his head and she was obliged to be his voice of reason. She cared for him too much to allow him to throw away this chance of success.

"We can find a way around this," Ryan said, following her into the hallway. "Let's talk it through."

"I'm done," she replied, walking up the stairs. "Please don't hate me, Ryan. I'm doing what's best for you."

She knew he was watching her walk away and she didn't trust herself to turn around. One of them had to be strong. One of them had to be sensible. And one of them had to ensure that Ryan became the man he'd always dreamed of being.

And if that meant she returned to being alone, it was a price she was prepared to pay.

ELEVEN

Sheriff Wilkins was visibly angry, standing on the sidewalk outside the Bethesda station, obviously waiting impatiently for Ryan to show up.

"You're late," he said, as Ryan stepped from his truck. "I said one hour and it's been almost two."

"I was busy," Ryan replied, no longer caring to show politeness where the sheriff was concerned. "Kitty's kitchen window got shot out yesterday and Shane and I needed to ensure that a new one was fitted before nightfall."

"I learned about that incident from Shane," the sheriff said. "We've got a homicidal man on the loose here in Bethesda, which is why I need you showing concern for the whole town and not just Kitty."

"But that makes no sense, Jim," Ryan said with exasperation. "It's Kitty he's trying to kill, so it's Kitty who needs me the most." He decided to lay all his cards on the table. "I met Harry Linklater today and I believe he's innocent."

"What's gotten into you?" the sheriff said. "Kitty's filled your head with all kinds of nonsense about a miscarriage of justice and you've lost any sense of reality."

"Actually," Ryan said, "there *has* been a miscarriage of justice."

The sheriff threw his hands in the air. "I don't know what to do with you, Ryan. You're wrong about this."

"I think we'll have to agree to disagree on that."

The sheriff pushed his hat back on his head. "Well, I'm glad to hear that you're moving out of the Linklater house. That's a positive step at least."

"How did you know that?"

"I got a call from Kitty a few minutes ago. She said she's cutting her ties with you and asked me to reconsider endorsing you as sheriff."

Ryan clenched his teeth together. Right then he was furious with Kitty for refusing to allow him to make his own decisions. She was trying to do right by him, but he didn't want or need her intervention. She should leave well enough alone.

"And I'm pleased to say that if you prove

yourself over the coming weeks, I'll be happy to support you once again," the sheriff said.

"Prove myself?" Ryan questioned.

"Do your job, serve the people and don't associate with the Linklaters outside of work." He raised his eyebrows. "That means no more visits to the prison, no more cozying up to Kitty and I definitely don't want to hear you repeat that you believe Harry is innocent. That's how you'll prove yourself."

Ryan stared at the sheriff, struggling to control his spiraling emotions.

"This is just one big popularity contest, isn't it, Jim?" he said. "You don't want me embarrassing you or making you look stupid."

"You don't need *me* to make *you* look stupid, Ryan," the sheriff retorted. "You're doing a pretty good job all by yourself." He instantly seemed to regret his cruel words. "Look, I'm sorry, but I'm under a lot of pressure here. I don't want to fight with you. The truth is that I need your skills here in Bethesda. I've got the district attorney breathing down my neck to solve the murder of the woman under the floor of the Starlight Bar."

"Do we even know who she is?"

"We got an official ID today, based on dental records." He pulled a photograph from his pocket and handed it to Ryan. "Elena Karowitz, a twenty-three-year-old Californian who drifted between states. She was quite a hippie, by all accounts, and she occasionally stayed in a commune up in the hills. She had a baby here in Bethesda before vanishing nineteen years ago."

All the clues pointed toward one person. "Buzz's mother."

"That's right. She worked for Harvey Flynn on a casual basis so it's no coincidence that she came to be buried under his floor. Her official cause of death can't be established, but there was a large crack in her skull. The rope used to tie her hands contained traces of Harvey's DNA, so we know he was involved prior to her death—he didn't just conceal the body. But her dress was stained with the blood of an unknown person who probably injured himself in the struggle. I want you to find out who that person is."

Ryan strongly suspected that the unknown blood would match Molly's killer. He had no idea how many victims were out there, but Elena, Molly and the girl found in the river were likely to be three of many.

"What was the name of Buzz's father?" Ryan asked. "He's Frank's son, right?"

"Tommy Price."

"Does anyone know where he is now?"

"I have no idea, but he's definitely a person of interest." The sheriff stepped forward and put his hand on Ryan's shoulder as if in a gesture of reconciliation. "This is why I need you, Ryan. Bethesda is reeling from the discovery of another murder victim, so I want it investigated quickly and thoroughly. And we also have to catch this gunman terrorizing Kitty." He raised his hands, fingers splayed. "I know I've been hard on her for monopolizing all your time, but her safety is still a priority. I need my best man on it here in town, chasing down leads—not hovering over Kitty down at the lake house."

Ryan nodded. He had to put their personal differences to one side in order to focus on serving justice. Whether or not he became the next sheriff was irrelevant. At that moment, he was a chief deputy and he had a job to do.

"I'm on it, Jim," he said. "You can count on me."

Kitty heard Ryan enter the hallway and take off his jacket. His presence in her home had become like a comfort blanket, but she knew it would be hard to adjust to living on her own again.

Ryan went into the kitchen and spoke with Shane. Their voices were low and hushed, as if Kitty were ill and in need of peace and quiet. She heard Shane saying that he was compiling a list of people in the area who owned the same make and model of boat that the suspect had escaped on, but it was the most commonly used vessel for locals and tourists alike. Both Ryan and Shane sounded despondent, as if the task of locating her attacker was overwhelming. They clearly needed help, but any extra assistance would have to be authorized by Sheriff Wilkins.

"The sheriff said you called him," Ryan said, coming into the living room. "And that you asked him to reconsider supporting me."

"I did," she said. "And I'd do it again a million times over."

"You told him you were cutting ties with me. Is that true?"

"Yes. I'll help you with the investigation and I'll work with you when we need to, but that's as far as it goes. We have to show the sheriff that you've distanced yourself from me."

"I don't need approval from Sheriff Wilkins for anything in my life. I don't even *want* to be the sheriff of Comanche County anymore."

"I can always spot your lies, Ryan, so don't try to hide from me."

He smiled. "That's what I love about you," he said. "I can't lie to you and I can't hide from you. You're the only person who really, truly knows me."

She winced at his mention of love. She didn't

want to drag this out, to make her heart ache even more.

"I called Nancy from the grocery store," she said, changing the subject. "And she says they have a spare room you can rent until you find something permanent."

He sighed and sat down. "You won't even take some time to think about this?"

"I don't need time."

"You said things would be different if we managed to prove your father's innocence."

"But that could take months or even years. You said so yourself."

"We got a breakthrough in the Starlight Bar murder case today," he said. "So we're already one step closer to finding the man who might've also killed Molly."

She sat up straight, intrigued. "What happened?"

"The woman under the floor is Elena Karowitz."

"Buzz's mom?"

"Yeah. Harvey's DNA was found on the rope used to tie her up, but we still don't know the origin of the blood on her dress. My guess is that it belongs to Tommy Price."

"You think Tommy killed Elena?"

"Yes, I do, and there's a reasonable likelihood that he's our serial killer."

"Nobody's seen Tommy in years. I don't think his family even knows where he is."

"Maybe they know more than they're prepared to divulge. Isn't it odd that he skipped town and never came back?"

Kitty barely knew Tommy, but she remembered him as a sullen and doleful young man, browbeaten by his father and spending much of his time at the Starlight Bar.

"Tommy was good friends with Harvey," she said. "And Harvey employed Elena as a bartender for a while, so he knew her well, too. Tommy and Harvey could've murdered her together and kept each other's secret all these years."

"That's what I'm thinking," Ryan said. "After giving birth, Elena might have wanted to take Buzz away, maybe even move back to California. Or maybe she just wanted to leave on her own, and Tommy didn't like the idea. Perhaps she had a fight with Tommy and he killed her, and Harvey helped conceal her body under the floor of the bar. Then Tommy pretended she'd left town, and because she was transient everybody just accepted his word."

"It's possible," Kitty said.

"It's more than possible. If Tommy killed Elena then there's a good chance he's gone on to kill others who look just like her. She was blonde and blue-eyed with freckles, like all the other girls who've gone missing. He could've developed a morbid obsession, seeking out young women like Elena to control and dominate."

"You need to talk to Frank," she said. "He's the only person who might know where Tommy is."

"I'm not sure that Frank is going to be very cooperative. He's made his feelings pretty clear."

"Shall we talk to him together?"

"I don't think your presence would help matters." Ryan rubbed a hand on his jaw, where stubble the color of a sunset had begun to grow. "Maybe we're barking up the wrong tree. Maybe someone else would be more helpful."

"Sheila?"

"Yes. If we could get her on her own, we could ask her what she knows about Tommy's whereabouts. It's worth a try."

"I think that Frank often goes to Carla's café for lunch," she suggested.

Ryan nodded. "That's right. I see him there every day at one o'clock, leaving Sheila on her own for an hour. We could try and sneak into the store while he's eating."

"Good idea. We'll go tomorrow. And then we can go see Nancy at the grocery store and get you settled in to your new place," Kitty said with forced positivity. "I think you'll like it there."

"I want to stay here with you. I won't be able to sleep a wink anywhere else, knowing you're here on your own."

"You'll get used to it."

"No," he said, rising from the sofa. "I'll never get used to it."

And in truth, neither would she.

Ryan moved quickly along the sidewalk, sticking close to the storefronts to conceal himself from the window of Carla's café. With Kitty close behind, they must've looked like a pair of criminals, scurrying from sight, but it was necessary to avoid Frank's gaze and find Sheila alone.

Ryan didn't even want to think about his suitcase in the back of his truck, fully packed and ready to transport into Nancy's spare room. His attempt to persuade Kitty to change her mind that morning had fallen on deaf ears.

Pushing open the door of the hardware store, he heard the bell ring overhead and saw Sheila look up from the counter. She smiled nervously as they approached.

"Frank says you're not allowed in here," she said. "But if you need something then I'll serve you real quick and you can leave before he comes back from lunch."

"We don't want to buy anything, Sheila," Ryan said. "We're searching for some information."

"Information?" She began to look even more uncomfortable. "What kind of information?"

"Did you know that the body recovered from the Starlight Bar was Buzz's mother, Elena?"

"The sheriff called yesterday to give us the terrible news," she said. "We're devastated. We had no idea she'd come to harm. We thought she'd moved on somewhere else."

Sheila's small eyes darted around as she spoke and her hand kept reaching to touch her curled hair, set with spray. Ryan could plainly see her anxiety.

"What gave you the impression that Elena had moved on?" he asked.

"Um…well, if I remember rightly, she told Tommy that she was too independent to be a mother and wanted her freedom, so she turned Buzz over to him and disappeared. We never saw her again."

"Where's Tommy now?"

"I don't know."

"When's the last time you spoke to him?"

"A long time ago—probably ten years or more. He decided to start a new life."

"Does he keep in touch with Buzz?"

Sheila shook her head. "No. Frank is the only father Buzz needs."

"Frank's not much of a father, though, is he, Sheila?" said Kitty, stepping forward. "He's a bully and he treats Buzz like a possession, the same way he treats you."

Sheila visibly shrank, as if she had been slapped. "Frank tries his best. He struggles with his temper and he's got some problems, but he can change with our help."

"If he hasn't changed in forty years, I don't think he ever will," Ryan said gently. "Why do you insist on making excuses for him?"

"He's my husband and it's my duty to stand by him," she said, pulling herself upright again. "I don't expect you to understand it, but that's the way it is."

Ryan saw that Sheila's eye bruise was turning a greenish color, though she had styled her hair to obscure the worst of it. Clearly, she had a warped view of a sense of duty. Being dutiful didn't involve being a punching bag.

"Do you have an idea of where Tommy might live now?" he asked.

"Why do you want him?"

"Why do you think we want him?"

She laughed, the sound high and brittle. "You think he killed Elena?"

"Did he?"

"No, he didn't. Tommy's a good boy, just like Buzz, and I won't hear a bad word said against either of them." She wrung her hands, becoming agitated. "You have no idea what we've gone through, but we still have each other. We're still a family."

"What have you gone through, Sheila?" Ryan asked. "If you tell me, I can help."

She fixed him with her steely blue eyes. "You can't help us. I think you should go now."

Ryan sighed and admitted defeat. Sheila was a closed book.

But as he headed for the exit, she called out, "Can I ask you something before you go?"

He turned. "Sure."

"How did Elena die? Do you think she suffered?"

"We can't say what killed her for sure, but there was a large fracture on her skull." He knew what Sheila wanted to hear, so he decided to give her the reassurance she was seeking. "It was likely a quick death. She wouldn't have suffered."

"Elena was no saint, you know," Sheila said. "But she didn't deserve what happened to her."

"What do you mean, she was no saint? What did she do?"

Sheila picked up a cloth and started wiping the counter. "I didn't mean anything by it."

"If you know something, you should share it,"

Ryan said. "You want us to find the person who hurt her, don't you?"

"I know nothing." She wiped the counter more vigorously. "Just leave, please."

Buzz appeared in the doorway that led to their apartment. "Is everything okay, Grandma?" he asked.

"Yes, it's all fine," Sheila said quickly. "Deputy Lawrence and Kitty just wanted to ask some questions, but they're leaving now. Perhaps you'd care to show them out, Buzz."

Buzz walked to the door and opened it, catching Ryan's eye. "Do you think my dad killed my mom?" he whispered.

"It's possible," Ryan whispered back. "The killer left a bloodstain on your mother's dress. If we can match that blood to somebody, we'll be able to make an arrest."

"Can you test my blood?" Buzz asked. "Would that help?"

"We don't need your blood. We just need a cheek swab for the DNA. That can be tested for a family link."

"What are you whispering about?" Sheila called from behind the counter. "I thought I asked you to show Ryan and Kitty out, Buzz."

"Come back tomorrow," Buzz whispered as they passed. "Three o'clock."

After stepping out onto the sidewalk, Ryan

steered clear of Carla's café and led Kitty a little way down the street before stopping.

"Well, that's interesting, huh?" he said. "If Buzz gives us his DNA, that will tell us whether the blood on the dress is Tommy's. And then we can try to establish his whereabouts."

"Sheila is scared about something more than we know," Kitty said. "I can see it in her eyes."

"I agree. That family is one big tangle of secrets." He glanced over at his truck, where his belongings were stowed. "I'll take you home, and come straight back to Bethesda to settle in to Nancy's house." He paused to gauge her reaction, but she gave nothing away. "Unless you've changed your mind."

"No, I haven't changed my mind."

"This is stupid, Kitty. You know it is. We can't let the sheriff rule our lives like this."

"You've already done so much for me," she said. "You have no idea what it means to hear you say that you love me. You're the first and only person who's ever given me total support and I'll never forget it. I owe you my unconditional support in return. That's why I've got to do this. I care about you too much to watch you throw away this opportunity." She reached up and touched his cheek, then she smiled and headed for the truck, seemingly carefree and untroubled, but he knew it was all an act for his benefit. If she was attempting to stop him from worrying about her, she was doing a terrible job. Wherever he went, Kitty was always at the forefront of his mind, and nothing she could say or do would rid him of his care for her.

"Okay," Kitty said, following Ryan around the house as he checked all points of entry. "I think we can assume everything is locked up as tight as possible." She checked her watch. "You should leave. Nancy will be expecting you, and I've got a news article to research for the *Tulsa Gazette*. It looks like at least one newspaper is still happy to employ me."

Ryan didn't let her distract him with her talk about work—if she had to guess, she'd say he was still focused on how to keep her safe without him there. He clicked his fingers as an idea clearly came to him. "I'll ask Shane to stay with you for a while, until we've got this guy caught."

"No, Ryan," she said. "It's not fair to ask Shane to risk his career. How do you think the sheriff would react? Shane would get into trouble and that's not right."

Ryan appeared to concentrate hard. "Is there anybody else who can stay here for a while? Any family members?"

Kitty had two uncles and a handful of cousins, and all had turned their backs on Harry—and her, by extension.

"My family doesn't want much to do with me anymore," she said. "So there's nobody I can call."

"What about a friend?"

She gave a hollow laugh. "You know I don't have any real friends, Ryan."

"Well, if you expect me to leave you here with no protection then you've got another think coming." He shook his head. "I'm sorry, but I can't do it. I won't go."

She had expected him to put up a last-ditch fight. "Yes, you will."

"You can't make me."

Kitty was reminded of the arguments she used to have with her parents when she was younger.

"Seriously?" she said. "You're really gonna start behaving like a petulant teenager?"

"You have no idea how hard this is for me."

Her chest heaved a little. "I think I do."

He pointed to the door. "As soon as I walk out of here, I won't be able to stop thinking about you. When I try to sleep tonight, I'll close my eyes and see you here alone, facing down a man with a gun. It's so stupid that I can't stay with you because of an election that I don't even care about winning."

She pushed him gently toward the door. "I'll

send you a text message first thing in the morning to let you know that everything is fine."

"Why don't I have another cup of coffee before I leave?"

"You had three already. Stop stalling."

She continued pushing Ryan to the door. He could easily overpower her and stand his ground, but he was allowing her to take the control she demanded. Kitty felt her heart wrench a little more at the way he refused to use his strength against her.

She opened the door and Ryan stepped out onto the porch. The light was fading and the lake shimmered like a painting under the early evening sun.

He stood on the porch, unmoving, so she closed the door, bolted it and called out, "You can leave now."

"I'll just sit out here for a while," he called back. "It's a nice evening to watch the lake."

His insistent care and kindness were wearing her down, chipping away at her resolve. She waited until she could be sure her voice was steady before saying, "I'm not letting you back inside."

"I know. You get on with your work for the *Tulsa Gazette*. I'm fine out here."

"But it's cold."

"It's beautiful," he said. "I could stay here for hours."

"You'll have to go eventually," she said. "You can't sit on the porch forever."

"I'll just watch the sunset and get on my way."

She walked into the living room and stood a little way from the window. Ryan was sitting on one of her wooden deck chairs, leaning back, with his feet up on the porch rail. She smiled at his posture of apparent relaxation. He was right about the lake—it was truly beautiful tonight. She longed to join Ryan and feel his arm slip around her shoulders. She wanted to sit like a couple of old folks with nothing more to worry about than raccoons in the garbage.

She backed away from the window, went to her desk in the corner and opened her laptop. Within minutes, she was trawling the internet for background information on the mayor of a neighboring county who was embroiled in an embezzlement scandal. Occasionally, she would look toward the window, where Ryan's feet were visible, propped up on the rail. Each time she saw those well-shined black boots she shook her head and smiled. He sure was stubborn. And she loved him for it.

Finally, as darkness folded around the house, she decided to take him some coffee and a blanket, so she rose from her seat and padded to the front door in her socks.

Opening up, she said, "Hey, you…"

She stopped. The chair in which Ryan had been sitting had been repositioned in the corner of her deck and was now empty. And his truck was gone. She felt her entire face fall as disappointment hit her in the gut. Why was she so hurt by his leaving? That's what she wanted, wasn't it? That's what she had *ordered* him to do.

The woodland beyond the house was dark, but she heard noises coming from there. Perhaps it was an animal. Nocturnal creatures often foraged in these parts once the sun went down. Yet these noises were humanlike: the rustling of leaves, the snapping of twigs underfoot…the shout of a man.

Did she just hear that correctly? Quickly stepping back inside, she slammed the door and locked it, her chest hammering. Should she call Ryan? This could be danger or it could be nothing.

She hopped on the spot, trying to rid herself of the anxiety and force herself to come to a decision. Finally, she walked purposefully into the kitchen to retrieve her cell phone. In her peripheral vision, she saw a piece of paper slide beneath the kitchen door and swish across the floor, landing close to her feet. Picking it up, she saw the word *RUN* written in big, bold letters, and spun around to try and catch a glimpse of the message writer through the window.

That was when she saw two wide eyes staring back at her through the glass.

And she screamed.

Ryan crept through the woods beyond Kitty's home. Only a few moments ago, while sitting on the porch, he'd seen a shadowy figure weave through the trees and had left his post to check it out. He intended to keep guard outside Kitty's home all night, no matter what she wanted. So after putting his truck in the barn to fool any intruders into believing she was alone, he'd telephoned Nancy to tell her that he was sorry, but he wouldn't be requiring the room tonight, after all. Then he moved his chair into a dark corner where he couldn't be seen. And waited.

He followed the sounds of a man's footsteps, kicking up the leaves and moving quickly, activating his flashlight to search the darkness.

"Who's there?" he called. "This is Chief Deputy Lawrence from the sheriff's office. Show yourself."

As he waited for a response, a woman's scream cut through the air like a knife, piercing him with terror.

"Kitty!" he exclaimed, racing back toward the house.

He found the front door locked from the inside, so he sprinted around back, gun in hand. His cell began vibrating in his pocket, but he ignored it, flying around the corner, to find Kitty's concerned face peering from the kitchen window. She was clutching her cell phone.

When she saw him, her eyebrows wrinkled in confusion and she opened the back door. "How did you get here so quick?" she asked.

"I never left," he said, running right past the door and into the backyard. "What do you see?"

She pointed to the field beyond, where a tall figure was sprinting. "He's running for the road."

"Go inside and stay there. I've got this."

Ryan set about his pursuit. He was an active man, kept fit by regular exercise. There was no way this guy would outrun him.

"I've got you," he muttered under his breath, chasing the man down, closing the gap more with each second.

When he finally got close enough, Ryan launched himself into the air and landed heavily on the guy's shoulders, bringing him to the ground in a tangle of limbs. There was shouting and kicking and resistance, but Ryan was firm and resolute, utterly determined that he would finally apprehend Kitty's attacker.

As he turned the struggling figure over on the ground, Ryan felt his belly sink in disappointment. He'd wanted his suspicions to be proven wrong. He'd hoped that the fresh-faced young man with the bullish grandfather would turn out to be decent, after all. But that wasn't going to happen.

Because the attacker was Buzz.

TWELVE

Ryan hauled Buzz to his feet and held him by the collar of his jacket.

"It's not what you think," Buzz said, panic flashing in his eyes. "I swear I wasn't doing anything bad."

"So why don't you tell me exactly what you *were* doing, Buzz?"

"I was trying to help Kitty."

"Help her? How?"

"I thought I could warn her," he said. "Someone's here and she's in a lot of danger."

Ryan's thoughts instantly returned to the man he'd been tracking in the woods. Where had he gone? Was he still there, staking out the house, watching Kitty?

"Who's here?"

"My father."

"Tommy?"

"Yeah. He's been back in town awhile."

"How long is a while?"

"I don't know, exactly, but he turned up at the apartment the day after I delivered Kitty's new door to you."

Ryan let go of Buzz's collar and grabbed his gun. "Where is he now?"

"I don't know. I followed him here and came around back to push a note under the door, but Kitty saw me and screamed. Dad might've run, but he might be hiding. We should go check on Kitty."

Ryan couldn't afford to take any chances on anyone, especially a member of the secretive Price family.

"You're not checking on anyone, Buzz," Ryan said, pulling handcuffs from his pocket. "You're under arrest."

But before he could secure the cuffs, a gunshot cracked the sky, and Ryan was forced to abandon his arrest and sprint back to the house.

Kitty fired a bullet into the ceiling. Crouched in the corner of her living room, she was trying to ward off the masked man who had just forced his way into her home. She had mistaken him for Ryan and opened the door, only to be faced with the barrel of his gun. She'd managed to slam the door in his face, causing him to yelp, but it had given her only a temporary reprieve.

He forced his way back in easily and proceeded to chase her around the house.

After failing to reach the panic room, Kitty had backed into a corner of the living room, raised her gun in the air and shot, hoping to scare her attacker into fleeing. But he stood in the center of the room, his own gun aimed directly at her.

"I don't want to kill you," Kitty said, pointing her gun at his chest with violently shaking hands. "But I will."

She didn't know if she had the ability to shoot. She had never so much as wounded anybody with her gun, let alone killed them. But her attacker seemed to have a similar sense of unease, a lack of desire to pull the trigger, and so they remained in a standoff. Kitty's heart hammered so hard that it physically pained her.

Then the man spoke. "I'm sorry, Kitty, but I have to do this."

At that moment the back door burst open and Ryan barreled inside, tackling the masked man to the floor. The two began wrestling for the upper hand.

Buzz appeared in the room, agitated and on the verge of tears.

"Stop it, Dad," he shouted. "Just give up."

Kitty thought she had been imagining things when she'd seen Buzz's eyes staring at her through the kitchen window, but here he was, calling her attacker *Dad*. Could this really be Tommy Price? When Ryan yanked off the ski mask, her question was answered. He was a little older and grayer, but the face of her attacker undeniably belonged to Buzz's father.

"Get Buzz outta here," Ryan yelled, as he grappled with Tommy on the floor. "And call Shane."

Kitty ushered Buzz away from the fighting men. Taking him into the kitchen, she heard frantic footsteps in the hallway. Tommy had broken free and Ryan was pursuing him out the front door. Buzz made an attempt to follow, but Kitty put a hand on his chest, pushing him back.

"You have to stay here, Buzz," she said. "Let Ryan deal with it."

"But Dad might get hurt."

"It's a little late to worry about that. He's made his own bed and now he has to lie in it."

"He's sick," Buzz said. "He needs help."

Kitty scrolled through the contacts on her cell to find Shane's number. "First of all, he needs to stop," she said to Buzz, waiting for Shane to pick up. "He's been terrorizing me for too long."

When Shane answered the call, Kitty quickly relayed all the relevant information, keeping her eyes on Buzz. The teenager was crying openly.

"Shane will be here in a few minutes," she

said to him, clicking off the phone. "And he and Ryan will want to ask you some tough questions, Buzz. Why did you push the note under my door?"

"I wanted to help you." He gulped, steadying himself. "I'm really sorry I couldn't protect you. I tried."

She pulled a chair from the table and invited him to sit. Buzz needed love and sympathy right now, not a judgmental attitude.

"You're a good kid, Buzz, and I appreciate whatever you've been trying to do for me. But you have to tell me what you know."

He took a deep breath, his hands clasped together on the table in front of him. "My dad came to stay with us a few days ago, right after your last newspaper article came out."

"Did you have any contact with your father before then? Your grandma told us that she hasn't spoken to him in ten years."

"She lied," Buzz said. "We go see him at least once a year. He lives in Texas now."

"Why all the secrecy?"

"I don't know. Granddad told me that it's no one else's business, so we're not supposed to tell anyone where Dad is. He's never visited us in Bethesda before. He says that this town is full of bad memories."

"So why did he come back?"

"For something bad, I guess. Since he's been back, Dad's been having secret conversations with Granddad about stuff."

"What stuff?"

Buzz appeared reluctant to say more.

"You should confide in someone, Buzz," Kitty coaxed. "You said yourself that your dad needs help. I can try and get him the help he needs."

"Dad and Granddad have been whispering about the night that Molly was killed, saying that no one will find out the truth if they get rid of Harvey and you. I heard Dad say that he'd get the job done, so I've been following him around, trying to warn you. I couldn't save Harvey, so I've been trying extra hard to save you."

"So it was you who painted the warning on my barn?"

"I thought you'd be safe if you left town," Buzz said. "Dad can't hurt you if he doesn't know where you are."

"Did he kill Molly?"

"I think so." He hung his head. "And I'm pretty sure there are others."

Kitty thought of the smiling faces of the missing young women in the photographs. "Others?"

"Dad and Granddad had a fight one night. Granddad said that murdering lots of women would mean a whole lifetime in prison. Dad got upset and said he wanted to go to the police and put things right, but then Granddad calmed him down and Dad agreed to get the job done."

Kitty couldn't quite believe it. "Your grandfather encouraged your dad to kill me?"

"Granddad hates you," Buzz said. "He says you poke your nose into our business."

"My father is in prison for the crime that your father committed," Kitty said. "That gives me every right to poke my nose into your business."

"I know it does, but Granddad just wants to protect the good name of our family."

Kitty couldn't help giving a snort of derision. "The good name of your family? You have the most dysfunctional family I've ever known, Buzz." She was immediately remorseful. "I'm sorry. That was mean."

"But it's true," he said quietly. "Dad and Granddad go around whispering and arguing about terrible secret things. Grandma pretends that everything is fine, but she knows more than she lets on. She just doesn't want to face up to it. When my mother's body was discovered, I could tell that Grandma wasn't shocked. She knew my mom was dead."

"How did your mom die, Buzz? Do you know?"

Tears filled his eyes again. "I was always told that she left town when I was a baby. I had no idea that she was murdered." He clenched his jaw, anger beginning to show. "I hate my dad for killing my mom. I wish he'd never come back."

Kitty put a hand on Buzz's shoulder. "We need you to help us," she said. "If you tell Ryan everything you know, he'll take care of you and your grandma. You don't need to be scared of your dad or your granddad. We can protect you."

"I'm not sure you'll be able to persuade Grandma to turn on Granddad," he said, his red-rimmed eyes filled with tears. "She's been obeying his orders forever."

"We can try."

At that moment, Ryan entered the room, approached Kitty and enveloped her in a hug.

"I'm sorry, but I lost Tommy," he said when he released her. "He vanished right under my nose."

"Dad knows these woods like the back of his hand," Buzz commented. "He grew up hiding from Granddad in the trees."

"Buzz and I have been having an interesting conversation," Kitty said to Ryan. "You should listen to what he has to say."

Ryan pulled up a chair.

"Okay, Buzz. Start from the beginning and tell me everything."

"There's no sign of either Tommy or Frank at the store or their apartment," Shane said, entering the house. "I got a cheek swab from Buzz for the DNA test. The lab will have a result for us later this morning."

He walked through to the living room, eyeing the clock on the mantel. "It's almost 9:00 a.m. Did you two get any sleep?"

Ryan put a finger to his lips. "Shh, Kitty's asleep right here."

Shane mouthed the word *sorry* and sat in one of the armchairs, smiling at his boss knowingly.

"Don't say it, Shane," Ryan whispered, as Kitty stirred gently in his arms, nuzzling her face against his chest.

"I wasn't going to say anything." Then he muttered, "Except that you two make a great couple."

Ryan ignored the comment. As far as he knew, Kitty hadn't changed her mind about any potential relationship. They hadn't really had the time to discuss it.

"She's exhausted," he said. "But at least we know who's responsible for all the recent attacks. Now we just need to find Tommy. Did you put out an alert to all officers across the state?"

"Yep, all done."

"Thank you, Shane. You've been picking up a lot of slack while I've been taking care of Kitty and I appreciate it."

"No worries. That's what I'm here for, right?"

"Did you talk to the sheriff?"

"I spoke to him about an hour ago. He wants to see you at the station this afternoon to talk about things."

"Talk about what things?"

"He didn't say."

"Does he know I'm here with Kitty?"

"Yeah."

"Is he mad about it?"

Shane shrugged. "I don't know. The sheriff's hard to read."

"He's a stubborn old goat is what he is," said Ryan.

Shane laughed. "Well, maybe he wants to apologize. We got Buzz's statement on record saying that he believes his father killed Molly Thomas."

"Yeah, but until we get some hard evidence, Sheriff Wilkins might not be willing to accept that." He shifted position and Kitty roused a little. "It took me long enough to admit that I was wrong."

"Listen, boss," Shane said. "Don't worry about it. You get some sleep and I'll stay with Kitty while you go see the sheriff."

"Thanks. I'll go to the hardware store straight afterward to get a statement from Sheila."

"Sheila?" Kitty said sleepily, waking up. "Is she okay?"

"Yeah, she's fine," Ryan said, rubbing a deep

crease on her cheek where the collar of his shirt had left an imprint. "We got someone to put a new lock on the door of the store and apartment. If Tommy or Frank try to get in, she'll call me."

Shane rose from his chair. "Looks like you two could use some coffee. I'll go make a pot."

Ryan smiled at his deputy, conveying his gratitude. Shane was excusing himself from the room to give the two of them privacy to talk.

"How long have I been asleep?" she asked, stretching her arms up high.

"About three hours."

"Best three hours' sleep I've had in a long time."

"Why don't you go to bed?" he suggested. "Shane will stay with you while I'm gone, and when I return, perhaps I could move my things back in to the apartment?"

She rubbed her eyes. "I don't know, Ryan. Have you talked to the sheriff about what happened?"

"Not yet."

"So you don't know whether he's changed his mind about you staying here?"

"No."

She shifted across the sofa. "Then let's wait awhile."

He took her hand. "You know it doesn't matter to me what the sheriff says, right?"

"It matters to me, Ryan." She stood up and yawned. "I think I will go to bed."

"Okay. We'll talk later."

She walked from the room, leaving the faint trace of her scent behind. Ryan sat quietly for a few moments, wondering what Sheriff Wilkins's viewpoint would be now that a new suspect for Molly's murder had emerged.

One thing Ryan couldn't quite believe was that his future happiness rested in the hands of the craggy-faced old sheriff of Comanche County.

Sheriff Wilkins stood by the counter in the Bethesda station, leaning against it with a satisfied smile on his face. Ryan was surprised to see him in such an upbeat mood.

"You look pleased with yourself, Jim," he said.

"I am," the sheriff replied. "I asked you to solve the murder of the body under the floor of the bar and it looks like you did it in super-quick time."

"Are you talking about Tommy Price?"

"I sure am. Shortly after you put out a warrant for his arrest, he was picked up by a patrol car on the state line. He's been taken to Lawton and charged with the murder of Elena Karowitz."

"Do we have the results of the DNA test?"

"Yes. The DNA in the cheek swab from Buzz has a family link to the blood found on Elena's dress. The blood definitely belongs to Buzz's father, so we've got our smoking gun right there."

"What about the murder of Molly Thomas? Can we link Tommy to that, as well?"

"I've decided to reopen the Molly Thomas case and take another look at the evidence. Based on Buzz's statement and the similarities of the rope in multiple crime scenes, it would seem that Tommy might not only be responsible for Elena's and Molly's murders, but a whole bunch of other women besides." The sheriff had the decency to look contrite. "I'm sorry, Ryan. I'm man enough to admit when I'm wrong, and it looks like I was wrong on this. We might have a serial killer on our hands."

"So you accept that Harry Linklater might be innocent, after all?"

"Yes, I do. And If Tommy Price turns out to be a serial killer, then his capture would be a huge case for me to finish my career on. Kind of like going out on a high."

Ryan suppressed his irritation. Sheriff Wilkins was typically using this awful case to glorify his own standing in the community.

"So this means that Kitty should be safe down there by the lake," the sheriff continued.

"Now that we've got Tommy in custody, she can sleep easy."

"What about Frank? He was aiding and abetting Tommy and he's not in custody, is he?"

"He can't hide forever. We put out a warrant for his arrest and I'm sure we'll pick him up sooner or later."

"I'm going to take a statement from his wife across the street," Ryan said. "I want Frank picked up sooner rather than later."

"Okay, you get on it. I'll call Shane to come back to work."

"But he's agreed to stay with Kitty until I get back."

The sheriff picked up the phone. "I already told you we've got Tommy in custody. Kitty's in no danger now." He punched in the number. "Good work, Ryan."

Ryan opened his mouth to protest, but the sheriff was already talking on the phone.

He left the station, deciding to hurry Sheila's statement and return to Kitty as quickly as possible. Frank's disappearance left him incredibly uneasy.

The door of the hardware store was closed and locked. He saw Sheila and Buzz inside, clearing the shelves, packing items into boxes. He knocked on the door and waved.

"Are you moving?" he asked, when Sheila opened up.

"I'm putting the store up for sale, and Buzz and I will be going to Georgia to live with my sister." She ushered him inside. "We want to be gone before Frank decides to come back. He's not welcome to come with us."

"Where is he? Do you know?"

"I have no idea, but I only hope that he stays away until Tuesday," she said. "I've finally decided to leave him, like I should've a long time ago. Now that he's gone, I feel lighter and stronger."

Ryan pulled a notepad from his pocket. "I really need to talk to you before you leave. I have a lot of questions."

"Like what?"

"Did you know that Tommy murdered Elena almost twenty years ago?"

Sheila glanced over her shoulder at Buzz. "Go upstairs, honey," she said. "And make some tea. I'll be up in a few minutes."

"Sure thing, Grandma."

Sheila waited for Buzz's footsteps to fade on the stairs and then she leaned in close. "Tommy didn't murder Elena."

Ryan put a comforting hand on Sheila's shoulder. "I know this is difficult for you to hear, but yes, he did. Buzz provided us with a DNA sample and it showed a parental match to the blood on Elena's dress. The blood belonged to his father."

Sheila took a big gulp of air, her throat visibly quivering. "The blood *does* belong to Buzz's father, but it's not Tommy's."

Ryan was confused for a second or two before he understood what Sheila was telling him. "Are you saying that Tommy isn't Buzz's father?"

"That's exactly what I'm saying."

"So who is the father?"

"Frank."

Ryan felt his mouth drop open in shock. "*Frank* is Buzz's father?"

"Shh," Sheila said, encouraging him to drop his voice. "Buzz doesn't know. When Tommy started dating Elena, Frank took a big interest in her and they got awfully close. I felt sure something was going on but I couldn't be certain, so after Buzz was born I sent away for one of those paternity tests. I got a cheek swab from Buzz and some of Frank's hair from a brush, and when I got the result it showed conclusively that Frank was the father."

"And did you confront him?"

"I confronted Elena first and she admitted that she'd had an affair with Frank. She said she wanted to leave town and take Buzz with her, but Frank wouldn't let her go. He was determined that she wouldn't take Buzz away from him."

"Was he determined enough to kill her?"

Sheila held the two sides of her cardigan together, as if warding off a chill. "Elena tried to leave in secret. She asked Harvey if she could work one last Saturday afternoon shift in the bar to help pay for her bus fare back to California, but Harvey called up the store and told Frank she was skipping town. He thought we should know." Her voice wavered. "Frank stormed off to the bar, murdered Elena in a rage and paid Harvey to help hide the body beneath the floor."

"How do you know this?"

"Tommy went to see her at the bar. When he got there, it was closed, but he looked in through the window and saw Frank and Harvey wrapping Elena's body in a sheet. He never got over it. He tried to stay strong for Buzz's sake, but Frank told him during an argument that Buzz wasn't his son, and after that, Tommy left town and swore he'd never come back." Sheila clenched her fists. "Frank destroyed our boy's life."

"But why didn't Tommy do something? Why didn't he go to the police?"

"Frank's always had a terrible hold over this family," Sheila said. "He's a violent bully and he's kept us in our place for a long time. Tommy always obeyed his father." She gripped

Ryan's forearm. "Will you please help me find a good lawyer for him? It's the least I can do after I failed him so badly, never interfering with Frank's cruelty."

Ryan's anxiety levels surged as he thought about Kitty. "Is that why Tommy's been attacking Kitty? Was it on Frank's orders?"

She nodded. "Frank tries to hide his actions from me, but I'm not stupid. He got himself a new gun recently and he disappeared after the town meeting, saying he wanted to stretch his legs. Tommy had showed up, right out of the blue, the day before, but I could tell he didn't want to be here. He was scared. Frank bought him a black car and ordered him to keep it at the warehouse, out of sight. He told Tommy to stay out of sight, too, and not talk to anybody."

"Tommy ran Kitty off the road."

"He never wanted to. You have to understand that Tommy is completely controlled by Frank. He's conditioned to obey."

"So Tommy didn't kill Molly?"

She shook her head.

"Who did kill her?"

The elderly woman closed her eyes, squeezing them tightly as if to erase memories from her mind. "I don't know how many girls Frank has killed in total, but I think it's a lot. He's always been drawn to young blonde girls just like Elena and—and…" She stopped for a second. "I just can't bear to think about it. He's got some kind of mental sickness that he can't control, and I've never been strong enough to stop him."

She opened her eyes and fixed them on Ryan. "I'm pretty certain that Frank killed Molly—just grabbed her off the lane, spur of the moment, after he dropped Buzz at the party." A tear slid down her cheek. "I'm so sorry."

Ryan turned and ran for the door. "I have to get back to Kitty."

He raced out into the street, saw that the station was closed, the sheriff gone.

Activating the siren and lights on his truck, he screeched away from the curb, praying that he was simply being overcautious. Frank was bound to have skipped town. He wouldn't be so stupid as to try and kill Kitty now. Would he?

Kitty opened the front door with caution. "What are you doing here, Frank?" she asked nervously.

"I hear there's a warrant out for my arrest so I'm here to give myself up." Frank appeared disheveled and wide-eyed. "I'd like to speak to Chief Deputy Lawrence if I may. Or Deputy Harmon."

Kitty kept her senses alert. Frank might not be the killer they were looking for, but he was still dangerous and violent. She took no chances, keeping the door open just a crack.

"They're not here," she said. "Ryan had to go see the sheriff, and Shane left a few minutes ago. You'll probably find one of them at the station."

"So you're alone?"

"Why do you want to know?"

Frank placed his foot in the small gap between the door and frame. "I just want to talk, Kitty. I want to apologize for everything I've said and done. Won't you let me in for a minute or two?"

She looked him up and down warily. "It's too late for apologies. I know that Tommy is a killer and you covered it up. This is a matter for the police now."

Frank smiled. "Oh, Kitty, you think you've got it all figured out, don't you?"

She swallowed away the lump of anxiety in her throat, pushed there by a rising sickness. Frank's tone had lost all pretense at being apologetic or nervous. Now it was hard, almost mocking.

"I *do* have it all figured out," she said, attempting a brave voice. "Tommy is a murderer and poor Molly was one of his victims."

"You've got it wrong, Kitty. If you let me in, I'll explain everything."

"That's not a good idea. Ryan is anxious to speak with you, so I suggest you head off to the station and see if he's there." She pushed on the door, trying to get him to move his foot. "I'm going to close the door now. I want you to go."

Frank's foot didn't budge. "Come on now, Kitty," he said. "All I'm asking for is a minute of your time and then I'll head straight to the station and sort this whole mess out."

"No."

She began to sense real danger in the air, as Frank stared at her with thinly veiled hostility. She exerted more force, trying to shut him out, with no success. She would not be able to prevent him from entering.

Then her cell phone began to vibrate on the hall stand and she glanced at the display. It was Ryan. She snatched it up and turned to run. If she could just make it to the panic room, she would be safe. It would buy her the time she needed.

Before she knew what was happening, the cell had flown from her hand, knocked to the floor by Frank's fist as he burst through the doorway. He shoved her and she fell, sliding across the hallway.

"Please don't do this, Frank," she said, as he advanced upon her. "It won't help Tommy if you hurt me."

"I'm not trying to help Tommy," he said, producing a length of rope from his pocket, exactly the same kind she'd seen in the pictures Shane had shown them. "He'll probably spill his guts to the cops and take a plea deal. He'd see his old man die in prison to save his own skin."

Kitty was confused and terrified. She had no idea what he was talking about. "Why don't we talk about this, Frank?" She was hyperventilating. "You said you wanted to talk, right?"

He smiled. "I changed my mind. Now I just want to see you die."

He gripped her wrist tightly, seeming to enjoy overpowering her. She tried to pull away but he slapped her face.

"You're not my usual type," he said, forcing her flat to the floor and attempting to wrap the cord around her neck. "I like blondes. But I can make an exception just for the chance to see you suffer. You've cost me everything, do you know that? Now I'll be exposed and it's all your fault. Why didn't you just die like you were supposed to?"

"No," she gasped, as he tightened the cord. "Stop."

Frank's jaw clenched and spittle gathered at the corners of his mouth as he put all his strength into choking her life away. Kitty's vision began to fade. She kicked and struggled, and one of her knees made contact with Frank's groin, causing him to double up in pain. She took her chance and scrambled from beneath him, then ran into the kitchen.

Yanking open the cellar door, she dashed through, slammed it shut and threw the dead bolt. After racing down the stairs, she started pressing the panic alarm button over and over.

"Please, Ryan," she gasped while pacing the floor. "Please come quick."

Then the bullets started pounding the door, one after another, creating an incredible noise inside the small space. She knew the door was reinforced, but had no idea how long it would hold.

The bullets suddenly stopped and she held her breath, waiting for something else to happen. Then a key turned slowly in the lock, sliding the heavy-duty mechanism. Only one other person aside from her had a key. The door creaked open to allow a shaft of light to fall on the stairs, a light shining in the darkness.

"Kitty, are you there?"

She let out her breath in one big exhalation and ran to the sound of Ryan's voice. There he was, at the top of the stairs, and she jumped into his arms, wrapping herself tightly around him. Lying on the floor of her kitchen was Frank, blood pooling beneath his prone body and his hands cuffed behind his back.

"You're okay," Ryan said into her neck. "I can't tell you how glad I am to see you're okay."

She didn't want to let him go.

"I've been torturing myself imagining the worst," he said, pulling away and cupping her face in one hand. "I don't know what I'd do without you, Kitty. You know I love you, right?"

She nodded, tears blocking her ability to reply aloud.

He didn't seem to mind her lack of verbal skills and continued to speak for the both of them. "And I think you love me, too?"

Again, she nodded as the tears streamed down, hot and wet. She heard sirens in the distance, heading their way, and she knew that her home would soon be full of officers and paramedics. She and Ryan didn't have much time together before mayhem took over.

"Yes, I love you, Ryan," she said, resting her forehead against his and lacing their fingers together. "I think we might just be made for each other."

Then she planted her lips on his and the whole world melted away.

EPILOGUE

Kitty fixed the banner onto the wall while Ryan held the stepladder firm.

"There," she said, holding his hand to descend to the floor. "All ready for Dad to come home."

She stood back and read the homemade banner aloud, relishing each syllable. "'Welcome Home.'"

Behind her, Ryan snaked his arms around her waist and kissed her neck. "You've done a great job with the decorations. Harry will love it."

"I hope so," she said, letting her head fall back on Ryan's chest. "I can't believe this day has finally come."

For the past three months, Ryan had been her rock, supporting her and guiding her through the legal process of launching an appeal against her father's conviction. When Frank was charged with multiple murders, including Molly's, Kitty had been approached by Sarah from the *Comanche Times* to break the story. The publicity it generated had propelled her journalistic work into a different league, and she was now being courted by national newspapers. Her name was becoming synonymous with a dogged determination to uncover the truth.

With the help of a great lawyer working on a pro bono basis, they had secured Harry's release from prison, and Frank was incarcerated. After recovering from his gunshot wound, he had been refused bail and had taken a plea deal, agreeing to life in prison to avoid the death penalty.

Ryan brought his lips to Kitty's ear and spoke gently. "There's something you should know. Shane telephoned a little while ago to tell me that Frank suffered a stroke last night. He's not expected to make it."

Kitty didn't know how to feel about this news. Frank deserved to pay for his crimes, but there was no doubt that his death would make it easier for Buzz and Sheila to move on with their new lives in Georgia. And Tommy would finally be rid of the last vestiges of his father's toxic influence, perhaps able to live a normal life at last.

"At least he led the police to the sites of the girls he murdered," she said. "He lived long enough to give their families some closure."

Frank had admitted to killing a total of fifteen girls, far more than anyone could have anticipated. He was a monster in their midst and she doubted that many residents of Bethesda would mourn his passing. Those who had previously treated Kitty with contempt now turned that bitterness toward Frank, and she had received numerous apologies. The most surprising one came from Carla, whose admission of wrongdoing was accompanied by a huge bouquet of flowers.

"It's almost time for us to leave," Ryan said, collapsing the ladder and stowing it away in the hallway closet. "You ready?"

Kitty took one final look around the room, festooned with decorations welcoming her father back to the home he hadn't seen in too long.

"I'm ready," she said. She reached out to Ryan and held both his hands. "Thank you. I'd never have made it this far without you."

"You got it the wrong way around," he said. "When I met you, I was carrying a lot of anger, and you showed me how to leave it behind. I'm not the same bitter person that I was when I met you. I should be thanking you."

"This is like a mutual appreciation society," she said with a laugh. "Let's just say we both helped each other."

He glanced at the clock on the mantel. "What time is your dad due for release?"

"Two o'clock."

"I'll get something from my room and be right back."

He disappeared into his apartment and Kitty stroked Shadow, who was weaving his way between her ankles.

"Today is a good day," she said to him as he purred happily. "We're coming home with somebody special."

"Okay, let's go," Ryan said, reappearing in the hallway with a sly smile on his face.

"What did you just go and get?" she asked him, narrowing her eyes in suspicion. "You look like the cat that got the cream."

"It's nothing."

"Nothing, huh?"

"I can't show you until I talk to your father," he said. "I like to do things the traditional way."

"Oh," she said, realization dawning. "So we might have a double celebration tonight?"

"We might," he replied, opening the door onto a bright and sunny day. "Let's wait and see."

She stepped onto the porch, planting a kiss on his cheek as she passed him. "Why don't we stop at the grocery store and buy a big party cake?"

"I'm one step ahead of you. I put one in the fridge already."

"You did?"

"Yeah, and I kind of invited a few folks over to join us later. I thought it would be nice."

"You invited people over?" she asked with surprise. She hadn't entertained guests at the house in a long time. "Who?"

He began to list people on his fingers. "Shane, Nancy, Paul, Joe, Carla..."

"Carla's coming?"

"Yeah. She said she'd bring her homemade cobbler." He clearly couldn't read Kitty's shocked face. "Is that okay?"

She smiled. "Of course. This is our community, right? And we have to forgive and move forward. Besides which, Carla's cobbler is legendary."

"Mr. and Mrs. Thomas have also asked to come along," he said hesitantly. "I wasn't sure if that would be okay. I said I'd get back to them."

A well of emotion bubbled inside Kitty. After spending so long outside the social circle of the town, she found the thought of being welcomed into the arms of Bethesda once again was wonderful. And Ryan had organized it all, even managing to bridge the biggest of divides.

"I'd be overjoyed to see them," she said. "And so would Dad. I can't believe you managed to invite all these people without me finding out."

"It wasn't easy, believe me. Even the sheriff said he'd drop by a little later on." Ryan gave an eye roll that spoke a thousand words. "He's keen to get started on my campaign for the sheriff's election." He laughed. "But I told him that I won't talk business today. Today is all about you and Harry."

"You're amazing," she said. "You'll be the best sheriff this county has ever had. I love you."

"And I love you, too, but enough with the mutual appreciation society. Let's get going."

She stepped out into the sunshine and raised her head to let the rays bathe her face. This was what it meant for light to shine in the darkness.

She had been delivered.

* * * * *

If you liked this story from Elisabeth Rees,
check out her previous books:

Caught in the Crosshairs
Lethal Exposure
Foul Play
Covert Cargo
Unraveling the Past
The Seal's Secret Child

Available now from Love Inspired Suspense!

Find more great reads at
www.LoveInspired.com

Dear Reader,

Thank you for choosing to read *Innocent Target*.
I hope you enjoyed the story.

Kitty is a heroine whom I admire greatly. She
stands alone, defying her critics and remaining
strong in the face of adversity. We could all take
a lesson from Kitty and fight for those who are
oppressed, imprisoned or written off as unwor-
thy. God has given us a voice. We should use it
to defend the weak, even if others do not always
agree with our stance.

Initially, Kitty and Ryan had a conflict that
could not be overcome. But as soon as Ryan softened his heart and let go of his preconceptions,
he was able to see Kitty's father as a man rather
than a monster. It was satisfying to see him grow
in faith and compassion through the story.

I look forward to welcoming you as a reader
again.

Blessings,
Elisabeth Rees

Get 4 FREE REWARDS!

We'll send you 2 FREE Books plus 2 FREE Mystery Gifts.

Love Inspired® books feature contemporary inspirational romances with Christian characters facing the challenges of life and love.

FREE Value Over $20

YES! Please send me 2 FREE Love Inspired® Romance novels and my 2 FREE mystery gifts (gifts are worth about $10 retail). After receiving them, if I don't wish to receive any more books, I can return the shipping statement marked "cancel." If I don't cancel, I will receive 6 brand-new novels every month and be billed just $5.24 for the regular-print edition or $5.74 each for the larger-print edition in the U.S., or $5.74 each for the regular-print edition or $6.24 each for the larger-print edition in Canada. That's a savings of at least 13% off the cover price. It's quite a bargain! Shipping and handling is just 50¢ per book in the U.S. and 75¢ per book in Canada.* I understand that accepting the 2 free books and gifts places me under no obligation to buy anything. I can always return a shipment and cancel at any time. The free books and gifts are mine to keep no matter what I decide.

Choose one: ☐ **Love Inspired® Romance**
Regular-Print
(105/305 IDN GMY4)

☐ **Love Inspired® Romance**
Larger-Print
(122/322 IDN GMY4)

Name (please print)

Address   Apt. #

City   State/Province   Zip/Postal Code

Mail to the **Reader Service:**
IN U.S.A.: P.O. Box 1341, Buffalo, NY 14240-8531
IN CANADA: P.O. Box 603, Fort Erie, Ontario L2A 5X3

Want to try 2 free books from another series? Call 1-800-873-8635 or visit www.ReaderService.com.

---

*Terms and prices subject to change without notice. Prices do not include sales taxes, which will be charged (if applicable) based on your state or country of residence. Canadian residents will be charged applicable taxes. Offer not valid in Quebec. This offer is limited to one order per household. Books received may not be as shown. Not valid for current subscribers to Love Inspired Romance books. All orders subject to approval. Credit or debit balances in a customer's account(s) may be offset by any other outstanding balance owed by or to the customer. Please allow 4 to 6 weeks for delivery. Offer available while quantities last.

Your Privacy—The Reader Service is committed to protecting your privacy. Our Privacy Policy is available online at www.ReaderService.com or upon request from the Reader Service. We make a portion of our mailing list available to reputable third parties that offer products we believe may interest you. If you prefer that we not exchange your name with third parties, or if you wish to clarify or modify your communication preferences, please visit us at www.ReaderService.com/consumerschoice or write to us at Reader Service Preference Service, P.O. Box 9062, Buffalo, NY 14240-9062. Include your complete name and address.

LI19R

MUST ♥ DOGS COLLECTION

SAVE 30% AND GET A FREE GIFT!

Finding true love can be "ruff"— but not when adorable dogs help to play matchmaker in these inspiring romantic "tails."

YES! Please send me the first shipment of four books from the **Must ♥ Dogs Collection**. If I don't cancel, I will continue to receive four books a month for two additional months, and I will be billed at the same discount price of $18.20 U.S./$20.30 CAN., plus $1.99 for shipping and handling.* That's a 30% discount off the cover prices! Plus, I'll receive a FREE adorable, hand-painted dog figurine in every shipment (approx. retail value of $4.99)! I am under no obligation to purchase anything and I may cancel at any time by marking "cancel" on the shipping statement and returning the shipment. I may keep the FREE books no matter what I decide.

☐ 256 HCN 4331   ☐ 456 HCN 4331

Name (please print)

Address   Apt. #

City   State/Province   Zip/Postal Code

Mail to the **Reader Service:**
IN U.S.A.: P.O. Box 1867, Buffalo, NY, 14240-1867
IN CANADA: P.O. Box 609, Fort Erie, Ontario L2A 5X3

READERSERVICE.COM

Manage your account online!

- Review your order history
- Manage your payments
- Update your address

> ### *We've designed the Reader Service website just for you.*

Enjoy all the features!

- Discover new series available to you, and read excerpts from any series.
- Respond to mailings and special monthly offers.
- Browse the Bonus Bucks catalog and online-only exculsives.
- Share your feedback.

Visit us at:

ReaderService.com